**Ann Rower** has always lived, worked and written in and around New York City. She is the author of a collection of stories, *If You're A Girl*, and a novel, *Armed Response*, published by Serpent's Tail. She has also worked with the Wooster Group and other performance ventures because she is a fan and likes to collaborate.

# Lee and Elaine

## Ann Rower

*Library of Congress Catalog Card Number: 2001087188*

A complete catalogue record for this book can be
obtained from the British Library on request

The right of Ann Rower to be identified as the
author of this work has been asserted by her in
accordance with the Copyright, Designs and Patents
Act 1988

First published in 2002 by Serpent's Tail,
4 Blackstock Mews, London N4 2BT
website: www.serpentstail.com

Typeset by Intype London Ltd
Printed by Mackays of Chatham plc

10 9 8 7 6 5 4 3 2 1

# ACKNOWLEDGEMENTS

Big thanks to the friendly ghosts in Green River cemetery for inspiring me – especially Lee Krasner and Elaine de Kooning and Hannah Wilke. To all my living sources – the East Hampton crowd, who let me into their lives and studios to tell me stories. Thanks to my friends who read versions of this book – Anne D'Adesky and Gay Bamberger, Diana Dietrich helped 'capture' it. Robert Jones was there, in the houses we shared and now will always be everywhere. Thanks to Frances Kuffle and the Jean V. Naggar Literary Agency, to Pete Ayrton and the Serpent's Tail crew, for their enthusiasm, to publicist Meryl Zegarek. To Rex Ray for the cover. Anyone who has worked with Amy Scholder knows no writer could wish for a smarter, sharper, cooler, warmer, deeper, more flexible, more feeling, thorough and thoroughly dedicated editor. She made work fun. Most of all, to Heather Lewis, who did everything, from line editing to removing herself from the plot for the sake of the ending. She always knew how to read me well. Whitney will always apply.

## DISCLAIMER

Although this book contains references to actual people and events, it is a work of fiction and should be read as such.

Earlier versions of two chapters, 'Baby' and 'Blur' have appeared in *More & Less* (Art Center College of Design, Pasadena, CA, 1999), and *Chance: The Catalogue* (Smart Art Press, Santa Monica, CA, 1996).

*For Helen Weinberg*

# *MISSING*

# *Death Kick*

January 31, 1993. As soon as I got out here, I bought the *East Hampton Star*. I picked it up at the IGA along with some groceries, then popped into the liquor store for vodka. One last stop – the video store for a rental – before I finally made it to the house in Springs, also a rental.

I tossed my stuff inside the door, then bumped up the heat to eighty. It was winter. The house had that empty cold. As I waited for it to warm up, I opened the paper. I stood at the kitchen table, flipping the pages, not looking for anything specific, just to feel in place, in the place, and suddenly there, on page one of section two, the Arts, was Hannah Wilke's obituary.

It was a shock. I never expected to see her so soon again. Not anywhere, but especially not here out on the end of Long Island, in East Hampton, in the *East Hampton Star*. I never associated Hannah with the Hamptons. I didn't recall her talking about going out for the summer. When I saw her, mostly she talked about how unrecognized she was. The full page article made me feel she had been wrong, that she was more important in the art world than she knew. That made me sad but I'm glad there's a picture. At the funeral yesterday, the coffin was closed. An obituary without a photo is like a closed coffin. Maybe this obit, and the one in the *New York Times* the day after she died a few days ago, were the beginnings of her finally getting her due. *The Times* even reproduced, on the opposite page, one of her drawings. I never saw them do that before.

Maybe you never heard of Hannah. I might not have heard of her either since I was so out of it, especially in the seventies, when it came to the art scene. But our paths always crossed, and kept crossing. One: we went to high-school together. Her name then was Arlene Butter. Two: we ended up living across the street from each other in Soho for twenty years. Three: we taught at Art University together and had many students in common. Oddly, my pets (student) always seemed to have trouble with her. We went to so many of the same events, shows, openings, especially her performances, where she, and audience chewer helpers, unwrapped and masticated bubblegum that she shaped into cunts and stuck all over her body. I wish she'd never changed media: lymphoma killed other women artists who worked with latex. Maybe she wouldn't be dead if she'd stuck to bubblegum.

Hannah died on Thursday, January 28. I knew she was very sick. Her sister said Hannah was having herself photographed, in the nude, as always; posing, as always, but no high heels, no guns, no tits and bush this time, just bloody bandages and bloody tubes blasting out of her, making drawings out of the hair she lost in chemo, the soiled bandages, her shunts, her holes, hundreds of slides, of her puffed-up hips, her balding twat – and everyone calls her a narcissist! We – Hannah and her sister and I – imagined the next show would include these, that it would be even more shocking than her last show, which was of her mother who was dying of cancer mugging vainly for Hannah's camera. We thought the new show would get more press, that Hannah would be at the opening because the show was going to be called "Cured."

I kept meaning to call. Maybe I would have been invited to

Hannah's wedding which had taken place – conveniently it turned out, for her new husband, who thereby became her executor – a few weeks earlier. But I'd put off calling as I always had, and I hadn't bumped into her new husband or sister on the street, which used to happen almost every day. A neighbor told me they all went to Texas for an experimental cure. Then, a few days later, I saw her *New York Times* obit. It'd hit hard that I hadn't seen her one more time. I called and at least got invited to the funeral. They told me the experiment failed, Hannah took a plunge there and died fast. Now they'd have to change the name of the show.

After the funeral the family and close friends had driven out to the cemetery, which they told me was in East Hampton. They'd asked me to come but it seemed too long a drive, and I always thought the graveside was for intimates. Then, too, by an amazing coincidence, I was coming out to Springs, the next day – today – right where the cemetery is, to stay in this house I'd rented so I could start writing. I'd said I would visit Hannah then, not knowing if I was lying, if I would or not.

But seeing this New York friend in the local paper made me feel strangely at home. And now I wanted to find her grave, her new place. Something pulled me there. So the first thing I did after putting the groceries away was to go in search of Hannah and the famous graveyard where all those famous people were.

Green River Cemetery. So many mid-century artists, writers, and critics rest, finally, with Hannah, here. The whole "New York School" practically: Jackson Pollock, Frank O'Hara, Willem de Kooning (oops, he's not dead yet), and the women, Pollock's wife, Lee Krasner, and Elaine de Kooning. I'd looked for this cemetery for years but I'd never had any luck finding it.

Now, finally, I had printed directions. And I was hot. Funerals always made me this way. They're so pornographic, they're orgies, and I'm a voyeur: all that spilled emotion, not just tears, shaking shoulders, arms around backs, all that hair, fingers, out of control faces. Our gynecologist (Hannah's and mine) who had a cunt piece of Hannah's behind her desk in her Soho office, was there, sobbing. I imagined it was because she couldn't save her.

I left the house with the directions between my teeth, pulled out onto Squaw Road, made a quick right onto Three Mile Harbor, and a left on Gardiner. I drove across to the other big road which runs parallel to "my" road, Three Mile Harbor – Springs-Fireplace Road – and turned left, then right at Ashwaugh Hall, drove past Pussy Pond, the Springs Store, past Deep Six Road, and turned onto Accobonac Highway. Before I knew it I was at the gates of Green River Cemetery.

I drove in slowly, with my bright red car blaring Whitney Houston. On the radio, in the air. I didn't love Whitney Houston but she sure could sing Dolly's old sweet song, "I Will Always Love You." I wanted to feel that way. I just didn't know who I could feel that way about. So every time it came on the car radio, I pumped it up. But as I drove through Green River, I realized this was way too much bass for any cemetery, even one with New York School bohos. I lowered the volume. There was only one other car there; then I saw one small cold family gathered around an old grave.

Once parked, it was easy to find her. I just looked for the freshest dirt. I knew, from the funeral directions, that Hannah was in the back part, the new part. The grave was right there, under my eyes. I stood looking down into a frame of grass, winter yellow dead, but with life in the color, the soil turned up like it does around earthworm holes. The freshness got to me. It was brownish wettish live red like someone rouged the mound, newly dug and put back, plumped like a blanket she was under. It was also the flowers. Someone must have left them on the shovelled earth the day before. They were still living – dying? – on her and I was unprepared for the way she moved me. Big tears popped out of my eyes by surprise – is that the motion part of emotion? I mean I loved Hannah. But she was impossible, a narcissist, and I don't mean her work. At her funeral, in the small Riverside downtown chapel on

Second Avenue, her dealer, Ronald Feldman, actually made everyone laugh and feel relieved when he mentioned right up front how obnoxious and self-involved Hannah was. When we'd bump into each other on the street, it would be an hour before I could extricate myself. Smart talk, interesting for a while but always all about Hannah. You couldn't interrupt, even to say goodbye.

Write about me, she always used to say. Her sister told me Hannah used to say, Write about me to her. I bet she said Write about me to everyone.

Green River Cemetery is hard to get into. Lucky for Hannah, Steve Ross, flamboyant head of fairly recently merged Time Warner, was dying when Hannah was. Steve must have wanted to merge not only the big print and screen giants but the producers and the artists by being buried with these other East End luminaries. Plus he must have had a place out here. I thought that was one of the requirements to be buried in Green River. Though I was sure if you were Steve Ross you could get around it. Or maybe you just had to buy a piece of real estate quick and turn it over. I'd have to check on that. I really had no idea who Steve Ross was, just a name recognition thing. Time Warner. Powerful. That they just called him Steve made me think he was young when he died. Or gay.

All I knew was after he died, his wife bought some land behind the cemetery and they'd forged a new group of one hundred and eleven plots down there, some of which were reserved for the Ross family. And I only knew this because I'd read an article about Green River Cemetery and how Streisand wanted to make a movie about Pollock. She wanted to direct it and play Lee, which caused a big stir, discontent among the locals, artists and otherwise, about Green River going so Hollywood. I guess Hannah got in because now there's room for a few other painters who don't object to Hollywood, either because they are dead, aren't anti-Semites, or because they love Barbra. I imagined somehow Hannah wangled a spot for herself.

But when did she arrange all this if she didn't believe she was going to die?

My first day at Green River, Steve was the only other identified person, besides Hannah, in the new back part. Near him were other stones, little boulders with no names waiting for other members of the Ross family. There was only one other grave: four film reels, stacked. No name. Very cool. I wondered, who is it? I should check. Someone must know.

I walked up the hill to the larger, more cramped old part, a flat rectangle filled with stones. Some dated back centuries, small and worn and tilted. Some were organized into squared-off family plots. All unknowns, at first, at least to me, until I, like Columbus, "discovered" them. Is voyeurism a form of imperialism? I thought it would be like Hollywood Boulevard's Walk of Fame, only the East Coast, East End version where you would actually be walking over real corpses, not just bought stars. But so far I'd come up empty.

The ground was fairly bare and brown but since it was only a month after Christmas, there were some decorations – some real, some fake. A white rail fence ran around three sides at the far end from where I stood, coming up the hill from the new part to the old. You could see Accobonac Highway and two ways in and out via a bumpy dirt road big enough for one car. I walked some more, looking for Lee and Elaine, but also – all right, I admit it – Jackson, Willem (oops), and Frank. But I couldn't find a single name I recognized. I was frustrated, but it was getting much colder and I couldn't stay anymore.

I walked back to the car, past a couple of big yellow boulders. My eyes were tearing from the wind so hard I couldn't even look at their names. The day got gray. Snow clouds were gathering. I was worried about the weather for tomorrow because I was expecting a visitor.

But I stopped to say goodbye to Hannah. I stood for a while. It was like bumping into her on Greene Street in the old days. Only this time I got to do all the talking.

# Elvis

You know how some people make you cloudy, and some people make you clear? Iris always blanked my head with fog. I never could think of a smart thing to say when I was alone with her, though some mornings in school I felt like I could shine for her only. I was so jittery, en route to the train station to pick her up. I hadn't seen her since our boozy talk at Lucky Strike over Christmas break when she told me she wanted to come out to visit me. How could I have been so stupid, so mixed up?

"It's Too Late Baby" on the car radio. "Something inside has died." I knew it was true. I had to leave him. Why was my pulse going so fast? Was it love? I loved my new house. Well, it's not exactly "mine." It's only a rental and I'm sharing it with my friend Bobby. He was trying to finish a book too, and we both were always complaining how we could never get any work done in the city – him because of his job and me because of the telephone. Or so I thought. This was my first real time coming out. I mean to the house.

The next song on the radio was about how I'm scared to

love you but I'm gonna try to be honest, and leave myself wide open to you, only it rhymed. I thought about Iris, about opening wider. It made me anxious, made my heart hammer again. I tried to convince myself nothing unusual was happening: a student I liked was coming out to take pictures because I happened to have access to water.

Maybe it was the car, the dangerous thrill of driving around, fast. I'm from the suburbs. I love driving, especially a red car, even a rental. Nothing is really mine. Maybe that's what I love. Is that sick? I skidded a little, taking a turn too quick, looking at the water not the road. I knew the roads weren't that safe. There had been many famous accidents out here. I almost did a Jackson – Jackson Pollock's drunk car tree Saturday night death on this same road. But I was struggling to eat a muffin, not slugging from a pint like he must have been, while juggling his scared girlfriend and her terrified friend.

Suddenly, to my left, I saw horses with the still unruffled bay shining behind them. Even in their rough winter coats they looked cold but not afraid. I swerved again, trying to get a better look at another farm, on another road, Three Mile Harbor Road, another real farm, not anyone's summer palace. A pig and a goat were out in their pen, rolling and cavorting. Their names, "Elvis" and "Priscilla," written large on the side of their barn. I wasn't a hundred percent sure who was who but I guessed Elvis was the pig.

I decided to bring Iris here from the train. It would diffuse our discomfort. Iris liked animals. Maybe she'd want to shoot them. With her Roli.

She wanted me to take pictures of her for this suicide project she was working on. She was going to do the Virginia Woolf bit – walk into the water, but unlike Virginia, naked. Since she'd have no pockets, she'd tie the stones to her wrists. I'd been dismissive, suggested she wait until spring, but she said she had to do it now, while she was in the mood. I didn't know if she meant in the mood to kill herself, or if the suicide thing was a game.

The water was freezing. Last week the bay had ice on it. Her insistence on doing the sea dip shoot in January seemed extreme. Iris was into extremes. I didn't know if this was part of a seduction plot so I could see her naked. I cursed myself for entertaining these thoughts. I'd sworn off sex with students years ago.

"It's such a violation," Jayne Cantor said. She teaches photography.

"Don't you think it's different if the teacher is a woman?" I asked plaintively.

"No," Marty White said. "Besides, it's illegal." She's a lawyer.

"Nancy Mess got fired from Pratt for fucking a student," Joyce said. She teaches at Cooper.

"Really," I said, my heart inexplicably pounding.

"They said it was for other things but really . . ."

"Really!"

"How could a teacher do such a thing? It's such a hideous misuse of power," everybody said.

"Yes," I nodded my head, disagreeing.

To me, not exactly dyslexic, things did get reversed from what most people thought. In the case of student–teacher sex, my feeling had always been that the student held all the powerful picture cards. How humiliating to have some beautiful strapping or strap-on youth bragging about this poor besotted professor who'd take their calls at midnight, buying all those stupid Stoli martinis and gourmet meals just for a lousy fuck. So I'd given up the practice years ago and tried to agree with my colleagues.

"It's very hard," Joyce said, "to face them in the classroom the next morning, after all those barriers to intimacy have been broken down."

"Besides," I said, "they tell."

Everyone snickered. I got panicky.

"It's true. They always do," Jayne said.

"But don't you think it makes a difference if the student is a woman?" I said.

They looked at me like I was crazy.

"If the student is an older woman?"

Iris was the first student, male or female, I could even imagine being on top of without squooshing to death in years. I loved that she was big. Bigger than me and almost as old. Well, I'd teased myself into thinking this.

I'd lie on the couch like a fourteen-year-old and imagine we could be friends. Then, when I let myself, maybe more. We'd be two glorious equals, running around the city, doing things, hearing music, seeing shows, holding hands. A gorgeous couple, her pale skin rosy, her short gray hair, my hair long and curly, many colors – I had no idea what color my hair really was by now. (It was not gray when I was her age. Maybe her gray let me convince myself she was older.) We'd be serious, but having fun, laughing, shocking people who'd be amazed I'd changed.

Iris and I had been flirting all fall but we'd only seen each other outside of school once, over Christmas break, at her insistence. She wore me down. I liked that. A movie, *The Crying Game*, then drinks at Lucky Strike and that talk during which the subject of our attraction, and my anxiety about it, had surfaced.

"What are you afraid of?" she'd asked.

I couldn't say it, not even now. I said the second stupid thing that popped into my head.

"That I won't get wet enough for you."

I must have been incredibly drunk. How could I have been that loose? She was my student. But earlier in the afternoon, before the movie, she'd gone into the ladies' room at the Angelika and came out licking her fingers. She'd stuck them under my nose. They'd glistened. They'd smelled. She'd smiled.

"See how wet I get?"

What was she thinking? I was her teacher. Why did I agree to let her come out to the house? In return she'd promised not to push. The second semester of class hadn't started yet and the first day always made me shaky enough without having to face a student I'd just slept with the night before, let alone a woman.

I was glad to have an excuse to stall longer, maybe forever. I didn't know what was happening to me, to my life. I sensed that the student/teacher issue was the least of it, yet it was the only one I seemed able, if unsuccessfully, to grapple with. Every time I told her how nervous I was about it, she said the right thing.

"It doesn't matter. I just want to get out there and take some pictures. I need to photograph the ocean. You're the only person I know with an ocean."

When I said I wasn't sure I wanted it to happen, admitted I was in total conflict about my sexuality, that I was still in a long-term relationship, with a man, how it would make it impossible to teach, spoil the class, she told me not to worry.

"I just want to shoot," she'd said.

I'd convinced myself it was true.

"It's going to be okay. Nothing's going to happen," she'd said.

"If you come, you can have your own room," I'd said. But then she'd glared.

I'd gotten anxious, retreated into confusion.

"For all your stuff, I mean."

She was bringing all this stuff out. A vintage 4×5 Polaroid camera, a big old wooden tripod, special developing chemicals for the Polaroids, her 2¼ Roliflex and her 35mm, too. I pulled onto Main Street – still as confused as I'd been at Lucky Strike, but miraculously not as tormented by the whole dilemma. Fate (death) had given me a reason to be grateful she was coming and bringing all her equipment.

I'd woken up this morning so excited, and couldn't tell which I couldn't wait for more, for her or to get back to Green River Cemetery with her. I wanted her to take pictures of Hannah's grave. If anyone could do it right, Iris could. She'd understand my desire to get that fresh dirt. And she'd known Hannah from Art University. She'd been Hannah's student too. Iris told me how on the first day of class, Hannah'd had them all sit there and watch while she'd shown hundreds of slides of her own work, including the one of her pissing. It was one of her best photos. She looked ravishing, peeing standing up, a golden stream shining, catching light. According to Iris, that whole sea of eighteen-year-olds forced to take Foundation Year Sculpture was disturbed. But, of course, not Iris, who was not eighteen.

My plan was that after I'd gotten her to shoot Hannah, we would explore the cemetery more. Get shots of Lee Krasner and Elaine de Kooning, if we could find them. I didn't know where Elaine and Lee were buried – didn't know much about them, except that they were painters who were more famous for being the wives of famous painters. I thought I had faint memories of seeing paintings by Lee and Elaine. This was when I was a kid and Action Painting was peaking. I remembered their work as similar to their husbands' work. I thought, hoped, wished they did it first; that the men had copied their wives' originality and then lied about it. That they were influenced by their wives' style and greater genius and got famous because they were men. That was my fantasy memory, but in reality, I could only see the men's work, the Pollocks and de Koonings; I could even feel their impact with my eyes closed. Especially with my eyes closed.

I turned up the car radio. I loved driving around Springs. Springs is like the Lower East Side compared to the Upper East Side or Soho which is East Hampton proper. Its biggest claim to fame was it's where most of the Abstract Expressionist painters came and settled in the forties and fifties. Pollock worked and died on Springs–Fireplace Road. The same road I was taking into town to meet Iris's train. De Kooning's studio was somewhere very near. On Woodbine, I'd heard. I must have just passed it.

But then, on the radio, a new song came on. I could breathe again, though it still felt like someone or something was driving the car. I began imagining the meeting, meeting Iris's train. I saw the train in the distance, saw myself racing wildly to cross the tracks before the signals started flashing and the bells started to ring. The gates started to come down, made my heartbeat race along with the motor. The winter trains were short, only a few cars. Not much in the way of people out here in the months after New Year's, before Easter. (Or Easter/ Passover, as it's celebrated in East Hampton.)

I fantasized how I'd wait, by the station, sitting in the car as people got off, with that wide-eyed, slightly anxious, slightly about-to-burst look in their eyes, searching – frantic, disappointed, let down, rejected – and then the connection: broad grinning, even squealing, hugging, though I could hardly imagine Iris squealing or hugging ever. I could imagine her stepping down, that then I would honk or wave, maybe get out of the car, make eye contact, approach. I could see her offhandedly saying hi and looking away, involuntarily.

But as I neared the station, there were no flashing signals, no bells, no train, no cars, no people. At first I thought I must be early. I started poking around in my coat pockets for lip gloss. Couldn't find it. Must have left it on the kitchen table. I needed it. I wanted to look good. Bad luck. Then I saw one lone figure, hunched over in a big leather jacket on the small bench in front with bags and tubes at her feet. Looking surly. The train was early. She was freezing. No time to look in the mirror. I was scared and apologetic. We were silent. I drove her to Elvis and Priscilla. She jumped out and for the first time seemed to connect. With the pig, I mean. And, to some extent, the goat.

I drove her to the calmest water I could think of, the bay at Three Mile Harbor, an absolutely magnificent curve to the pebbly shoreline, and at the end, where it began to go out of sight, a giant deep red clay cliff rose up, grass at the top, a house.

"You're crazy," I said.

"I want to do it."

"Tomorrow's supposed to be warmer."

"I have to do it now."

She began to take off her clothes, then stopped, stooped down and opened her bag. She had ropes in it and three huge rocks.

"You brought them all the way from the city?" I asked.

The beach was loaded with boulders.

By now she'd taken off everything. Then she put her leather jacket back on. Her nipples were pink and hard, from the leather and the cold. Her breasts were fabulous, I'd seen that the first September morn she'd walked into class, in a tight white tee-shirt and black jeans, striding in, flopping down into a seat, giving me a look. I'd looked back. She'd looked away.

She held out her bare cold arms and handed me the rope and the rocks and said "Help me."

# The Bathers

We rushed back to the car. I turned up the heat and tried to drive fast because she was freezing. She couldn't stop shivering, but was trying hard not to as she pulled on her clothes.

"Thank you for letting me come out," she said.

She said thank you a lot. I admired that. It was a good habit. At the time I didn't realize it was butch manners.

"I think the pictures are going to be great," I said.

I swung the car into the noisy gravel driveway. Because the snow had melted since this morning, it crunched so loud I thought I'd run over something. It scared me. Her teeth were still chattering. I couldn't get the car heat going strong enough.

I pushed her up the steps and ran a bath. I put in bubble bath, lit the "tranquility" candle from Zona, both of which smelled good. I'd bought them yesterday after Hannah. Not for her, for me, I'd thought. I moved in and out of the room. She stood around, awkward, frozen. A small tub, the pressure excellent, it filled up quick.

"Go on," I said. "It's ready."

She strode into the bathroom, still in her leather jacket and banged the door tightly closed. We hadn't looked at each other in a while, maybe not since she stepped off the train.

I heard her sigh, splash, moan a little. I wanted to open the door a sliver and peek in. I tried to think of a smart comment, something I had to tell her right away but my mind went into mashed potato mode, plus I thought she might yelp in fright, or snarl, or tell me to get out. It was hard to imagine her inviting me in. Hard for me to imagine, I mean. I wasn't even thinking of the tub. Not until right then. Then I was afraid she'd say, "Come in." I'd open the door and sit on the toilet. "No. Come into the tub, silly old thing."

Old? Though it still sometimes felt like she was close to my own age, I realized that just meant she was over thirty-five. She didn't think we were the same age. She was right, of course. But to me it felt like we were almost the same, two adults, only I was the teacher. Which was odd. She'd already teased me meanly about being too old to change: to give up my comfortable life, the way things were. She'd said it fiercely, her eyes bright, her skin getting even pinker. She was so passionate about everything. Maybe I wanted to get closer to her because I thought her passion would rub off. She even gave me Jeanette Winterson's *The Passion* and red-lined a part about Odysseus being tied to a mast not to hear the lure of Circe's song, so I didn't open the door.

I wandered around the house. I'd been here many times over the years, to see my friend Alex Germaine, writer and editor and now my landlady. Recently Alex had added on the second floor with a balcony water view. Then she had the whole house painted yellow. These improvements meant she could rent it out to pay the mortgage. The money came from the summer tenants. This was the first year she'd even thought to rent it in winter. And she'd offered it to me first. I knew I couldn't afford it, but the pull was so strong. And when Bobby agreed to share it, that brought the cost down to $350 a month, still high for me, but it was only for five months – until Memorial Day when the summer renters, as yet unfound, would start paying that many times over.

There was only one condition of getting to rent the house at this price. Eventually, probably when the weather got better, Alex had said, I'd have to show the house or let the realtors come and show it. If I showed it, I'd have to clean – whip out the Windex, get lots of shine – and then hype the house. If the realtors brought clients, I'd still have to clean, but then I was supposed to disappear and let them hype. Most crucial, Alex assured me the realtors would always call first.

Renting this house was just what I thought I wanted. To get away, to write, to be alone. But now having Iris here felt even better. Then worse. Had I gone to all this trouble, come all this way, spent all this money, to have a place to have a secret affair? I tried to distract myself from having such a bad thought. So I went through her things.

In her bag were not only all her cameras, film, some books, her journal, underpants and socks, but a huge grocery bag of food: salmon steaks, two jars of artichoke hearts, a box of farfalle, a container of heavy cream, a quarter pound of butter, a can of black olives, salad stuff, olive oil and vinegar. How could she afford it? At Lucky Strike, we'd talked about food. She'd said if I let her come out, she'd bring all the food. She'd talked about artichokes and asparagus.

"You do like artichokes," she'd said, like it was a threat.

Lucky for me I could still eat anything.

"I'll show you how to eat the heart," she'd said, picking up her knife and slicing an air heart apart.

"I know all about artichokes," I'd said, sounding huffy, shifting gears, my teacher voice coming out. I'd hated myself, but had no control over it. She'd scared me. But it had worked. She'd been put down. It had showed in her face. Everything showed in her face though she tried hard not to let it. I'd felt

bad. I hated that teacher in me. It made me feel old so I'd
made myself soft, got the conversation flowing two ways again.

"Everyone's different. I put a plate on top to keep them
from turning up in boiling water. How do you do it?"

She'd let my question hang a beat.

"You'll find out."

I'd gotten nervous.

"It's not artichoke season," I'd choked. "It's a spring food.
You'll never find them."

"I'll bring artichokes in a jar. It's all hearts. It'll be spring
soon. I'll bring real ones next time. And asparagus."

Next time?

I spread all the food out on the living-room couch. I looked
at the fish and the rest of the stuff and wondered how much
had they cost? Before, en route to the water, we'd stopped for
a minute to get extra film at the little store and when we got
back into the car she tossed me a container of Häagen-Dazs
she'd stuck under her jacket. First I thought she'd been
rehearsing for the frozen water she was aiming to enter. Then
I realized she'd thieved the pint. I didn't know how broke she
was. The first, the only time out, the Lucky Strike time,
she paid. I'd thought that was going to be part of the pattern.
It turned me on. A student who paid. And she did insist on
bringing dinner. But now I got a little chill, wondering did she
steal all that too? What happened to the ice cream? Where was
it now?

I ran back out to the car. Of course it was still there, under
the front seat. Still frozen. The sky was deep sharp purple,
hard and cold. My eyes filled with tears from the weather.
They ran down my face. I wanted to run back in and stick my
head into the bathroom and make her think I was crying.

I tried to think of a reason to open the door. I should ask
her if she wanted me to refrigerate the cream and butter and
salmon but then she'd know I'd been in her bag. Suddenly my
pulse went fast again at the thought of being caught. What
she'd do to me. I put everything back quickly. I heard her

stand up, pictured the water running over and down her skin, saw water beading on her pink and white flesh. I heard her splash as she got out of the tub. I hoped she wouldn't notice I'd rearranged things.

Looking around the kitchen, I saw the massage oil, which I'd bought along with the bubblebath. I'd spent an hour in the health food store, called Second Nature. Opening bottles and jars. Peppermint, almond, eucalyptus, sesame, things with names like Passion, Euphoria, Golden Touch, Rosy Aura, Heavenly Glow. The smells had aroused me, like smells do. The words had embarrassed me.

I'd put the massage oil where she'd notice, right next to the vodka. When she opened the bathroom door she wore my white terrycloth robe, held tight up to her neck though it was already firmly sashed. She squatted over her suitcase and pulled out a sweater, new underpants and jeans.

"Are you hungry? I'm gonna cook now," she said.

"What are you making?"

"Grilled salmon and butterfly pasta with olives and artichoke hearts in a cream sauce."

I thought about the fat content of this meal and realized maybe I was afraid of getting involved because I don't want to take my clothes off for her. For anyone new. That I felt, not what I thought – old – but fat. Possibly old and fat?

"What?" Iris asked.

I didn't realize I'd shuddered.

She stood up and carried the food into the kitchen. I followed her. I caught her eyes catch the vodka and massage oil.

"Can I help?"

"No."

"I'll make the salad."

"No. I'm doing all of it myself. I want you to relax."

It felt like an order.

She put the load down on the counter.

"But you can use my bath water. I didn't get it that dirty,"

she said and whipped off the big white French terry robe and
held it out to me.

"Take it."

# Sweets to the Sweet

The next morning we left for Green River Cemetery before nine. My mother had always warned me about living in the country: no privacy. In the country you never knew who was going to stop by, or pull up asking for directions or to use the phone, walk right in sometimes, without knocking or knocking but you didn't hear because you were out back. I heard my mother's words faintly on the way out the door, glancing over my shoulder at the empty wine bottle, Duraflame log wrappers cast about with food particles on the flokati rug, ashes strewn around the fireplace. And the Häagen–Dazs container. Heath Bar Crunch. But I was half asleep, and mostly happy nothing really happened last night. I backed out of the driveway. Crunch. I almost hit a tree.

Dinner had taken four hours to prepare because she wouldn't let me help. After we ate, we watched *The Player*, the video I'd rented, and had the ice cream she'd stolen. Iris had a sweet tooth. It might have been the only sweet thing about her she'd shown so far. I used to like Heath bars as a kid, and would perversely suck the chocolate coating off each bite and then spit out the toffee because enough of its sweetness was on the inside edge of the chocolate wavy jacket. But now they put it in ice cream. We sat on the floor and I fed the fire and Iris fed me. I had to lean way forward to lick the spoon. But just as my tongue was about to get there, she jerked it back a little. It surprised me. She threw her head back all the way and laughed. I felt a flutter of anxiety, almost fear. She stuck it toward me again and pulled back again. Nasty and playful, drawing me closer and pulling the spoon out of reach at the last possible second. Again she held it out. But a little closer. I was pulled a little closer. Pulling away, reaching, till little by little we were almost licking the spoon together, almost kissing. Then we did. One sticky kiss. But that was it.

I was hoping Hannah would still be wet and open, the ground still disturbed, the flowers still alive. Iris got busy setting up her tripod. She wanted to try the Polaroid, the special 4×5. We had containers of solution to slip them into until the negs were brought back to the house, taken out of the solution in darkness, hung up in the cool dark basement to dry. On the beach she'd just used the 2¼ Roli, and she would use that for Hannah, too. But she also wanted to experiment, wanted something more technical, or magical, or more malleable, something she could manipulate, an unknown. I tried to hold the tripod and get the plastic containers ready but she didn't want my help. I backed off, roamed around, looking for Lee and Elaine, Jackson, Willem (oops), old Frank O'Hara.

I didn't usually read poetry, but I liked Frank O'Hara because it wasn't like poetry. He wrote a poem I loved about Billie Holiday, called "The Day Lady Died," because they called her Lady Day. The poem was about seeing her photo and the *Post*'s big black headline at a newsstand in Murray Hill and I remembered that exact thing happening to me in real life the day Jimi Hendrix died, his face on the *New York Post*, the big words, the same newsstand in Murray Hill. I found out about Hannah by flipping routinely to the obituaries and seeing her face. And then did it again, in the *East Hampton Star*. It's such a shocking way to find out, but I loved that, when someone you know is on the obituary page and you didn't know they died.

So we shot Hannah, got Hannah, then wandered around, looking for the other bigger names. It was so cold. I'd heard O'Hara was buried at Pollock's feet, but we couldn't find either of them. Iris in boots and leather, me in a raggedy politically incorrect Persian grey lamb jacket I found in Alex's closet but would've never dared wear in the city, we started roaming around looking for other names we could recognize but without success. All we found were some dead veterans. We got back in the car, discouraged.

As we pulled out, something caught my eye. You couldn't miss it (though I had), a big stone with an ugly patina'ed blob on it.

"Look," I said, stopping short. "I bet that's somebody."

"Of course it's somebody," Iris said, mocking me.

"No, I mean somebody famous. It's so big."

We stopped the car right in the road – there was no one else there – and ran over. It was Elaine de Kooning. The green ugly swirling vortexy mass seemed dropped onto the polished pink granite like a big cow plop – meadow muffins they called them in Vermont. The sculpture on the stone was unattractive. I wondered who chose it, designed it. Willem? Then I thought about how Green River was not far from where de Kooning still had his studio, that he was still painting paintings he didn't know he was painting. He'll be here soon. Next to Elaine. I'm glad I found her.

I tried again to remember what Elaine de Kooning's paintings looked like. The image of them that floated up in front of my eyes were paintings that looked more like Pollock's, only smaller, tighter, more condensed. I hadn't thought of that possibility, that Bill de Kooning was influenced by Lee Krasner and Pollock by Elaine de Kooning. Why not, since they all must have mingled at parties, foursomes, double dates, riding around drunk in cars.

"Ug-ly!" I said, looking close at the stone.

"Was Elaine a dyke?" Iris asked.

I was shocked. "What makes you say that? She was married. To Willem de Kooning."

I didn't know why she'd said that. Was that a thing dykes said? About everyone?

"What difference would that make?" Iris said. "Especially back then?"

"I don't know."

Why did it confuse me so? Was it because I knew nothing about Elaine de Kooning and felt stupid? Or was it something more?

"You should find out," she said.

# Deeper and Deeper

When we got back to the house it was afternoon. We took the plastic containers with the special solution sloshing around downstairs and clipped the pictures to the clothesline. The one of Elaine's gravestone looked beautiful. The tone of the print was warm dirt, earth brown like Hannah's earth, clear brown velvet, sepia for some reason, maybe having to do with the chemicals or the 4×5 film, an antique medium. The image in all that, though, was sharp and clear, her name, scrawled like her signature, the blob, the flowers, the white fence behind her. Perfect. It was beginning. The project. I remember in college studying Heidegger. We were told that the word "project" in *Being and Time* was not an arts and crafts thing, like a Martha Stewart segment, but pronounced like pro – as opposed to amateur – pro-ject, accented on the first syllable but sounding more like something that projected you in time, with your expectations and its unknown complications, or as in projectile vomit. It did seem to link us into a future, like a module links up with a spacecraft. But I still wasn't sure how far I'd allow myself to go, or how hard she'd push, or what planet I'd end up on.

"Thank you for letting me come out," she said.

"You have to make me my picture."

I'd taken the shot she wanted of her naked walking into the water with the boulders hanging from ropes tied around her wrists. I'd also taken some other pictures, before she'd undressed, hunched over, back to me and the wind, in her black pants, black leather jacket and gloves, and I wanted her to superimpose the two shots, the two Irises.

"I wish we'd found Lee Krasner," I said.

"She should be right next to Elaine."

"I think that spot's saved for Willem," I said, trying not to sound like a snotty know–it–all.

"I could make them side by side for you."

"He's not dead yet."

"No, I mean Elaine and Lee. The girls. Isn't that what you want?"

I got goosebumps. "I guess," I said, hugging myself and rubbing my arms to warm up. I didn't know where any of this was coming from. Or going.

"I don't even know where Lee is?"

"We'll find her. Next time."

Next time? I panicked. Again. She sounded like she owned the house, had plans for every weekend. It made me mad, nervous, and confused. So I got up. After a while I calmed down and came back.

"Thank you for Hannah," I said, copying her butch manners.

"I can't believe," she said, yawning and stretching her arms back over her head so her breasts stuck out and up under her leather, "you went to high–school with Hannah Wilke."

"Arlene Butter."

"Why didn't she keep that name? It's so sexy."

"Maybe she didn't want to seem like a joke."

"Did you know her really well?"

"Well . . .," I said, thinking that all I knew about her then was that she was a cheerleader and really sexually experienced. I never thought of her as arty. She was too pretty. Other people called Hannah a slut, not us, of course. We were artistes. We put experience in general and sexual – as well as chemical – liberation above all other traits. I knew Hannah from having taken a "purity test" with her in high-school. Purity tests were clearly ambiguous. You wanted to score high and low at the same time. You were asked all kinds of broken-down questions starting with kinds of kisses – on the mouth lips closed lips open below the neck above the waist above clothes under clothes but above bra under bra without clothes below the waist and so on down to all the way. You started with a hundred, the "pure" score, and got points taken off for every yes. Then everyone had to read their scores aloud. Hannah got the lowest. I felt ashamed to have scored so high. My score would have been much better if I had counted my experience with Grace, but I didn't. Somehow the wording of the questions and my own repression forbade it. Clearly that was not what was meant by "going all the way."

"Fucked up," Iris said when I told her this.

I'd already mentioned Grace to Iris. It was that same one time at Lucky Strike after the movie when I was spilling. I guess I'd thought Iris would be more intrigued if I had some experience with girls. But not too much. So I'd emphasized how long ago it had been, how Grace was practically – chrono-logically – a girl when we met. We were both thirteen. We met at an arty camp on the Cape. The first summer we were just close friends. The second, closer. My mother used to send care packages of Gruyere cheese in little foil triangles and Triscuits. We'd sneak out of our rooms and away from our roommates into the woods, sit on the ground, talk all night, till four in the morning. She had a thrilling big low voice. She was in theater. I was in dance. One night we went back to her room, got in her bed, a few feet away from her sleeping roommate. I thought I was the virgin – I'd never had anyone else touch me like that but it turned out she'd never even come before. But I'd never told Iris any of the details, just that I'd had a girlfriend when I was a teenager. She said, "I knew it."

Because Iris did not come out of the blue. But she did come out of the green, as in Green Mountains, as in Vermont, as in more than six months ago, Labor Day, the exact day before my first class of the autumn semester, the class Iris was in. Looking back, it seemed to have happened in a moment, overnight, the night I'd spent, those many months ago, fifth wheel in a house full of same sex couples, of different sexes.

Once again we were up in Vermont, in Grace's beautiful old farmhouse. Jack and I had been going there for summers, and, as always, I'd always liked staying through Labor Day and then having to rush back down to the city the day before school started, partly so I could put off going back to work as long as possible, partly so I could go into my first class tan. This time Jack had wanted to leave early so he could be with his mother, who'd gotten suddenly more frail over the summer, and I'd wanted to stay and besides, Grace and her girlfriend and two friends of ours were coming for the weekend and they could drive me and the cats down with them, which would make things simpler. So I'd put Jack on the bus and stayed on by myself and driven back with Grace the day before school started.

By the time I got back to New York and started teaching twenty-four hours later, with this woman student, Iris, sitting in the front row, in her tight white tee-shirt under her black leather jacket, I'd already started doing things I never did before. Before Iris, I hadn't looked at a woman in years. No, I'd looked. I'd even looked twice and looked away. But never, not since Grace, back when I was fourteen, did I make a move. That's what, with Iris, was new. In class, I'd given an exercise to show how journal came from the word *jour*, to mark off a twenty-four-hour "day" on paper and fill in twelve things you did during this period, one of which was not true.

My list.

1. Woke up in Vermont, gray, nervous about leaving, the trip, the cats, getting back but missing Jack.

2. Heard Grace and Joan, the women whose house it is, having sex in the old squeaky bed and took off my clothes and ran in and joined them.

3. Terrified the cats would escape and we wouldn't be able to leave, and so they would stay calm, I locked them in my bedroom and went down to pack my computer, got to talking and drinking coffee, two hours later went back up. Heard the alarm buzzing, realized it had been buzzing all that time because I woke up earlier than it was set for and was so anxious about everything I'd forgotten to turn it off when I went down so I left the cats freaking in a closed room with the alarm on and I started freaking, like it was a very bad sign, how spaced I was, felt terrible.

4. Stopped at the General Store to say goodbye. Felt teary and pleased to be missed. Where's Jack, everyone asked. I explained he'd gone home to be with his mom on the holiday. I wanted to stay and he wanted to go. First time we settle an argument by agreeing to go our separate ways.

5. Total rush of Green Mountain bigness and lushness I was leaving.

6. Ate my last peanut butter and fluff sandwich I will ever eat outside Hartford.

7. Can't believe it's hot, noisy, crowded; yesterday it was quiet green cold and I don't feel anything different.

8. Saw Jack standing in front of the loft, biting nails, waiting for me, felt a rush of affection seeing him.

9. Stood in the loft and felt weird that it didn't feel at all weird, just a shift, now I'm here, then I was there.

10. Had smoked trout and red wine at Ear Inn.

11. Remembered I left my bag with all my shoes in it in Vt.

12. Had a dream I was in the shower and holding note cards

for class and the water washed all the words off and swirled them down the drain.

Looking back I must have taken one look at Iris and decided on #2, my fake entry, showing that you can lie to tell the truth, like the line in one of my favorite songs "Ain't It Peculiar," "If truth makes love stronger how come lies make mine last longer." Not that I didn't always like to give some kind of message to students that I'd some interest in women. For two reasons. One because it was true, and two because it made it easier for the lesbian and gay students to come out in this surprisingly homophobic art school. But this seemed awfully direct, especially for me, especially on the first day when I usually tried to be neutral. The idea was the class had to try to guess which was the fake one – a device designed to make everyone try to listen harder. Someone guessed it. I blushed. I looked at Iris, but she was looking away. What was going on? Was I coming out? Or was it still the fake one? But it had to be real: this experience I had in the country, this overnight sensation, my green thought in a green shade . . .

"I'm going to send your picture to Hannah's sister."

"Hannah has a sister?"

"Yes," I said. "Her name is Marcie. She gave up her shrink practice and her whole life, kids, everything in Los Angeles and moved to New York to take care of Hannah. I bumped into her at the health food store one day. That's when I knew Hannah was very sick. I didn't recognize her. She was in my creative writing class senior year in high-school. I didn't even remember her. Maybe she'll send me the picture of me and Francie."

"Francie?"

"Did I tell you I went to my high-school senior prom with Francis Ford Coppola?"

"A million times."

I felt humiliated.

"That's what we all called him," I said to cover my embarrassment. "Francie."

"Hard to picture."

"He was very thin."

"She has a picture of you and Francis Ford Coppola? In high-school?"

It had been hard for me to believe it too. Hannah's sister had said she had a picture of me and Francie on the night of the prom at her house, where we had stopped for a pre-prom party. She said I was in a beautiful white lace strapless, and Francie was in a tux with a plaid cummerbund. He was so thin it swam on him. I drew a complete blank. Maybe I remembered the dress. I dyed white satin heels red-scarlet. I was thrilled about being able to document this story I'd been telling everyone for years. It made the rounds. Recently some student I didn't know that well rushed up to me in the hall and said "That thing about you and Martin Scorsese is awesome."

We were sitting watching the cardinals flash down into the feeder. I laughed, as always, a little proud but also embarrassed, especially with her, because it dated me.

I'd asked Hannah's sister to send the picture to me when she got back to Los Angeles. She'd looked at me so strange, like that meant Hannah was going to die. But she did give it to me after she came back to New York a week after Hannah's funeral. I went up Hannah's loft to get it. Ceramic cunts were still arranged all over the floor. I'd been so excited, thinking about having a picture of me and Francis Ford Coppola at our senior prom. I'd have proof. I imagined how much pleasure I'd get by casually showing it around, though I still didn't even remember going to her house for a pre-prom party. I couldn't even picture myself at anyone's senior prom, let alone mine. All I could think of was Sissy Spacek in *Carrie*.

"Here it is," she'd said.

I'd looked at it hard. There it was. What there was of it. Of me. At least I thought it was me. I was standing with my back to the camera. My hair was in a flip. Was it my hair? I must have had it done. You couldn't see my face or really tell it was me, but the dress had nice, white lace tiers. I remembered the shoes. Scarlet satin. Blood red.

She pointed.

"See?"

There next to me there was a shape, a vague figure inside a soft rectangle, at best maybe someone sitting on the back of a couch, possibly the back of a white jacket. A small white blur.

"That's Francie!" she'd said.

"Right," I'd said, sunk.

There was nothing there. I knew I was not going to get any celebrity points with that shot.

"You have to show me the picture," Iris demanded.

"You know, Francie had a thing with Hannah. Later. He still calls her Arlene."

"Really."

Then it got quiet. Iris got up and put on "Deeper and Deeper" and started dancing. I felt my stomach curl. She turned it up. I got more anxious.

"Let's go upstairs again. The light's so nice up there."

We went up the stairs. I went first. I felt her eyes on my ass.

This second floor, added last spring, had skylights and a little porch. I walked over to the big double doors and looked out. The trees were bare, tangled, full of birds, two pairs of red cardinals. You could see water through the branches; the ad in the *East Hampton Star* could truthfully say waterview.

She joined me at the doors to the teeny new balcony. She turned me all the way around. I thought she was going to kiss me. It was one of those French doors with many panes. I backed against it. I imagined my head going through the panes of glass and either slicing my neck and having to be rushed to the hospital, or dying, and her having to call and break the news to Jack. It'd be in the *East Hampton Star*. Or, at the very least, add to the nightmarish condition of the house, which by now looked like two mad women lived there. My head whipped around. I breathed in hard, then realized she was trying to get me out of the way so she could take a picture of the branches. I turned back. My gaze went outside a window, not really seeing, picturing Wednesday's class. The first class. I could visualize her smirking, everyone knowing. Had she told? Did she need to? Had I given myself completely away? I panicked, thinking how much I was giving way, bending our vow about it. They all already knew. It was completely humiliating. I dashed downstairs and ran around, looking around, seeing every misplaced object magnified.

There were the Polaroids – she'd tried to photograph me naked on the rug the night before, after my (her) bath. I'd let her. What's wrong with me? The pictures were hideous. Maybe she was too close. Maybe it was a technical thing that made me look all blurry and wide. A big white blob. A whale. How could she want to fuck me if I looked like that? How could I even have such a thought?

I ran faster. The kitchen looked insane, like things do when you're tripping. The stove was coated with massage oil. The sink was full of empty bottles, vodka and wine. What should I do? How had I gotten myself into this mess? I couldn't wait to get back to the city, my ordinary life. This was a mistake. I just wanted to write. Right? I felt hopeless, helpless, homeless. My mother was right. About country life. Waaah. I wanna go home.

# Home

But when I got home, he looked like a stranger. Like someone I didn't know anymore. I didn't know I'd gone so far away. But it wasn't the miles, or even the time.

He didn't like my going away, but he was totally accepting of it because he wanted me to finish my book as much as I did. Of course I hadn't told him I was starting to think about working on a different book, about Elaine and Hannah and the other women buried in Green River Cemetery I hadn't found yet. I hadn't told him I'd had company that first weekend. Let alone a student. He hated when I got to be friends with my students.

I had lived there with him almost exactly as long as I lived with my parents. It was interesting because when I was young and living in the burbs, all my freedom had to do with the city. But now I needed another place, the country, the beach, another season, winter (there are no seasons in the city, really, like it's always night, with lights on). Actually, I needed both. I felt like I needed both of everything. But maybe I was splitting apart. I felt like I did when I was young and leaving home, torn by sneaking into the city on the Long Island Railroad to see Grace because my mother had forbidden it. This was after she found the love letters Grace had written to me, tied in a bundle in the top drawer of my desk. Grace thought I should be mad at her for snooping but I wasn't, I was mad at me. How could I have left the drawer wide open, the letters right under her nose that way unless I wanted to be found out but was too chicken shit to tell my mom the truth? Was it happening again only now it was the country? At the other end of the Long Island Rail Road line? It was Iris. A girl again. Did I want to be found out again? Or just found? Who would catch me now? Jack?

I lay awake awhile. He fell asleep before me with a smile on his face. His hand on my leg. Close. Like we used to sleep. Maybe my going away was alright. Right. For the right reasons. Maybe I could keep doing it and keep coming back. Keep going back and forth. One of the cats, then the other, joined us in bed. His hand moved away from my thigh to pet them. I snuggled in close to Jack and let the purring pull away the anxiety.

Home was such a comfort. That was the problem. Part of it.

"You were snoring," he said when I woke up halfway through the eleven o'clock news. I was totally humiliated. I felt like some old drunk or something. (In fact, I had secretly taken some pill for sleep and I did read somewhere that sedatives make you snore.) I struggled to find words, to ask to hear the worst, because I knew he would be candid. He was never a big communicator, but he didn't lie.

"How do you feel when I snore?"

"It makes me feel good," he said. "Then I know my girl-friend's home."

# *Absence*

Unable to go back to sleep, I tried to think about tomorrow's class. A lesson plan. Immediately I had to can the idea of "the most intense thing that happened to you this week" warm-up exercise, since I hate lying to my journal.

"You have to tell him," she'd said, after he called me out at the yellow house that first weekend. She'd heard me say on the phone I was getting a lot of work done, how good it was for my book to be alone, though I missed him so much. She glared at me when I hung up. I hated her hearing me lie.

"I will," I said, thinking now I was probably lying to her even more, hoping she wasn't planning to tell the whole Fine Arts Department. I suspected already that she would show everyone the photo she took of Hannah or someone would see it in the darkroom and have to ask. Or the photos I took of her walking naked into the sea. But so what? Nothing happened. She took some pictures. She was a photographer. She took pictures of women. That was her speciality. I was getting interested in women. Some of mine were dead.

I took another pill. I'd think about it tomorrow. I fell asleep.

It was a good sleep, deep, peaceful, the kind of sleep they say you have if your conscience is clear. Or dead.

I woke up feeling okay. Ready to face the music, so long as it wasn't "Deeper and Deeper." But when I got to class, Iris was absent.

# Lie

I panicked. Maybe she couldn't face it either. Maybe this was good, though I was dying to see the pictures she took: Hannah, the Polaroid of Elaine, the double exposure she'd promised to print for me, superimposing the one I took of her in her leather and the one of her naked with stones tied to her wrist walking into the freezing water. But I didn't call, didn't try to find her. But I couldn't stay home either. I couldn't wait to get back to the yellow house, maybe try to get the floor fixed, be alone.

And I wanted to go back out and look for more people in Green River Cemetery. I wanted to find Lee Krasner. By myself. I thought about what Iris'd said about Elaine. Who knows? The only thing I remembered hearing about Elaine was how many people she fucked, supposedly to advance Willem's career. Maybe some of them were women. Gallery owners? Betty Parsons? Peggy Guggenheim? Maybe I'd uncover some deep dark secret that'd always been buried. Iris would be pleased. I imagined that moment. Her I-told-you-so smile, like she looked when I told her about Grace. The thought of how wide she'd grin scared me more. I tried not to think about it. It made me want to get away from her too. I looked at the speedometer. I was going eighty-five. That's the trouble with rentals. They're so new. The bare trees looked wicked, dangerous, flashing by. I slowed down, tried to calm down, convince myself she was just a student, which she still was. Not still was. Was. Nothing happened. I mean, not really. Except for that quick sticky kiss. Well, I mean, if you don't count the massage.

"I want to give you a massage," she'd said, a little bit after we finished the Häagen-Dazs, that first night she was in the house.

I'd never had a massage, I'd confessed that earlier night at Lucky Strike. So now I felt I had something to prove.

"I can't believe you never had a massage."

I felt very fucked up, again. I imagine that she'd had and given thousands of massages in her life, to hundreds of people. That she was a pro.

"No. Not even at the beach. No one ever rubbed my back. No one ever offered."

"And you never asked?"

I was full of shame and confusion, but for some reason I felt I had to be honest. It was the least I could do. The most. Was it because she was a girl?

"No."

I never asked for anything. Never learned. Is that what being an only child is all about? It ruins you. They don't call it spoiled for nothing. I had difficulties bringing other things to the surface as well, like tears and rages. Maybe massage would bring out more feelings, bring the inside feelings out, closer to the surface, bring happiness and sorrow, passion and dejection, surprise and pensiveness, a parade of feelings, a fleeting flower, a flowing river, pouring out through the pores? Would it get me in touch with myself? Like the signs on the country roads: HIDDEN DRIVES. Was it too late, baby? Too late to feel? I needed to open, but I was not a flower. Would a massage do the trick? Would it lead to sex? I stopped myself sternly. That's your problem. That's all you think about. Was it all those years with all those men? I was looking for something different. And it was so hard to admit it.

"Just a massage. Not to worry," she'd said. "I want to give you one now."

Was that less than a week ago?

I'd tried to act cool.

"Wait a minute," she'd said. "I forgot something."

She clomped back downstairs in her boots. While she was gone I took off my clothes, got into bed, and pulled the sheet up over me. I felt like an idiot, a bride in a Merchant Ivory movie.

She stomped back up, holding the bottle of Kiehl's massage oil. She sat down on the bed and pulled the sheet away. They say you can't smell vodka on anyone's breath but there was a sharpness in the air.

"Turn over, baby, give me your beautiful back."

For some reason I was not worried about my future with this woman. More importantly, I wasn't worried about my big ass. This woman knew what she was doing. She knew I was too shy to have sex with a woman for the first time in years and too nervous to have it with a student right before the first class of the second semester. And she knew that to expose my breasts and my bush frontally too soon would be too much.

"I'll be right back."

"Where you going now?"

"Relax."

I heard the rattle of pots and pans. Then a faint odor, slightly acrid, partly sweet, more rattling.

"Fuck. Ow!" Iris howled.

"What's wrong?" My voice was shaking a little. Iris came back upstairs. Her face was red and sweaty. She looked a mess. There was oil all over her shirt. She turned off the light quickly and straddled my back. She poured the hot oil on.

"Ow!"

"It's supposed to be hot."

I wanted to believe her. She seemed so sure. I wanted that. Technique. It seemed sexy. I bit down hard into the pillow. She rubbed, kneaded and swirled, the slickness on skin, the extreme warmth felt better, made me happy, except for this little gnawing feeling that wouldn't go away, which I couldn't tell her about.

After she finished she stood up and went away. I took a look over the other edge of the bed and knew exactly what had happened. She'd heated the oil to warm it, like you're supposed to, to body temperature, but was probably a million miles away in thought, or thinking about what she was going to do to me, and the oil bubbled up and got way too hot, the way only oil can get too hot, to the temperature that's perfect for french fries or doughnuts but she didn't know this about oil. If she knew that much about cooking, the dinner prep wouldn't've taken four hours. Then still not thinking, she tried to pour the oil back into the bottle like nothing had happened. When she did, the plastic collapsed. But she didn't say anything. She brought it in like that and put it on the floor where it was now, all bent over to one side. It looked like a small Henry Moore sculpture, in the middle of a pool, a huge oil stain on the brand new floor. I'd never be able to scrub it off. Alex was going to kill me. I'd ruined her house. So much for the new addition.

An animal darted across the highway. I was still on the Long Island Expressway. My heart thumped till it was safe. I have a lot of dreams about animals in the road and I'm trying not to hit them, young soft baby ones. A shrink I went to three times thirty years ago said I was dreaming about my own vulnerabilities. I remembered how the cats jumped up on the bed and snuggled together in between me and Jack. Was it last night? Time was all mixed up. It darted across my mind that I must be crazy to be driving in the opposite direction from all that. "I Will Always Love You," again on the car radio. That crappy modulation always filled me up with every kind of feeling and no-feeling. I thought about her. I thought about him. I thought about the cats. I got pulled over by a Suffolk County cop wearing a lavender tie for speeding. Everyone did seventy on the Long Island Expressway. Why me? If only they didn't call it the LIE.

# My Funny Valentine

So I went back and forth, which seemed sexy to me.

"Are you ever going to let me come out again?" she said when she called.

"Yes."

"Are you ever coming home?" Jack said when I called him.

"Yes."

Class was still on track, which seemed miraculous to me.

"Aren't you going to stay home this weekend?" he'd said, sweetly, watching me zip up my computer. "It's Valentine's Day."

"I need to work."

"Why can't you work here?"

"The phone. Too many phone calls."

"If you wouldn't let your students call you at all hours, you could work here," he said and walked back into his studio.

As he turned, I could see part of his face: I changed my mind, unzipped my computer and went into my room to work.

I was trying to finish the old book. I'd been working on it for almost as long as I'd been with Jack. It'd been his idea.

Shortly after we moved into the loft together my uncle, who was a big Hollywood songwriter, died. I remember the night it happened. The phone rang at two in the morning.

"You know, you should write a book about him," Jack said the moment I got back into bed. "You could talk to everyone in the family, get all the stories, it'd be great." I was excited immediately. A great way to deal with death. It sounded so practical. So commercial. So much fun, unearthing the family secrets. I knew I could get them to talk. If I was writing about it, it'd be a way of connecting. When I went out to LA with my mother for the big Hollywood-style funeral I was insecure, nervous about leaving Jack, afraid I'd come back and find him in bed with a dancer, though I had no real reason to think that. But as I started working on the book more, lining up more Hollywood people to talk to, I started going away more. Jack was so supportive of the idea of the book that he didn't object.

But, instead of the biography, a novel came out about those trips and all the creepy funny stuff that happened in my family while I was out there supposedly researching my uncle's life. That was easy for me. The bio was hard. I couldn't get the tone. What came out was sing song, like I was writing a children's book. Maybe because it was about my family. Maybe I was trying too hard to keep the anger out. All the while my uncle's wife and kids and Jack and what was left of my mother's family kept asking, Where's the book? So I was desperate to give it one more shot. That was the whole point of renting this house. To please the family, and especially Jack. I guess he seemed like family now, too. It seemed to annoy him that I'd ended up writing "fiction."

But now, already, I felt like I wanted to write another book, about other trips, this time about my visits to Green River Cemetery, the women in Green River Cemetery. To have an excuse for them (the trips), like the Hollywood bio became an excuse to make those trips out west. It seemed very mixed up. I didn't know if I had to get away to write, or if I had to be writing about something to get away. To get away with it.

Something didn't feel right but I didn't know what was wrong.
I felt like a song lyric, but not "My Funny Valentine."

# Green River

I had no more visitors. I knew no one. At night mine was the only light on for miles. "Aren't you scared?" people said.

Bobby told me the first night he was here alone, he took a break from working, walked into the kitchen to fix a vodka and there was a young Latino boy standing there in just a white tee-shirt and tight jeans on a bitter cold night, shivering, wanting to use the phone. Fantasy? I believed him.

Sometimes I missed the city, missed Jack, missed the cats. Sometimes I missed Iris. But he'd said who wants to go to the beach in the winter and when she'd been here I got no work done at all. After she left, I'd drifted, disturbed, in a fog, sometimes coming out of it and bumping into a wild happiness that lasted a moment, ten minutes, a whole CD, then back to black again.

I tried working on the old book, and made some progress, but the trip to Green River was what really got me out of bed each morning. I'd begun thinking how Hannah had a lot in common with those other women in Green River I was dying to find. Hannah, like Elaine and Lee, was involved with a power artist of another generation. She was always in his shadow, always getting betrayed, screwed, ignored by him. She was with that big, in every way, pop guy, Claes Oldenburg, for years. I imagined maybe she influenced him too, that she was already making those beautiful little sculptures, pieces of shit, or were they cocks, or little cunts, and he might have said to himself, well, if I just make the same kind of thing only instead of little, I'll make them big. And instead of using human body parts and organic material I'll use soft plastics and make giant spoons and telephones, because that'll be easier to get. Maybe Oldenburg even talked Hannah out of making giant vaginas. Who knows. I did hear she was in love with him – maybe partly because he had power and she wanted power. Supposedly she adored him and lived happily, secure and domestic, with him. Then one day she came home. It was probably late afternoon. She had bags of groceries, a bottle of wine, a nice dinner in mind. The locks had been changed. She had no idea. Oldenburg, turned out, got married that morning. To someone else.

For months after she'd put her signature bubblegum vaginas on his mailbox. They were so clean and sweet-looking, even after when she made them out of latex and ceramic. Maybe Hannah chewed all that sweet Bazooka because she was so bitter. She felt that being a woman artist kept her from getting the attention she felt she deserved. And even worse, other women artists, especially ones who used vaginal iconography, somehow ended up being more famous, though Hannah was doing her early cunt pieces while the others were still doing what Hannah called "boy art." She always felt ripped off by them, the others who were less confrontational, less obnoxious, less involved with presenting the personal female. It got her in trouble, left her isolated, unpopular with some women artists who thought Hannah was trying too hard to be glamorous, or even that she was too glamorous. This made it hard for her to be taken seriously as an artist.

Hannah was the first artist I visited in Green River Cemetery, the youngest grave and body. But the minute I saw Hannah, found her there, I started thinking about Elaine and Lee. It was like all my history and attachments to Hannah shifted, and hooked onto Lee and Elaine in a bigger way than I could understand then.

I wondered how Elaine and Lee felt about being married to their big competitive icons. But even more, I wondered how they felt about each other. How this affected their friendship? What was it like being women artist friends? I assumed they were friends. They were always so peripheral in all the stories about those wild men and wild times, always mentioned as Pollock's wife, de Kooning's wife. Suddenly I wanted to find out about these women. Find them, period.

I turned off the car, got out and slammed the doors too hard, a thing I do. It woke up the dogs in the house in the back of the cemetery where I parked. I'd wondered who lived there. Was the house connected to the cemetery? Two typical East End Bonac Labs wiggled over. One dog was black, one blond. I petted them before going to see Hannah, where I always went first. I was still not sure what the pull of Green River was but I was here again. Was it, like my trips to LA, the pull of dead stars?

After Hannah I went to visit Elaine. She was my second "discovery," my only other destination. Was it finding her with Iris that made her so intriguing? When I saw a picture of Elaine she reminded me of Hannah, the same delicate-boned pretty face. I still hadn't found Lee Krasner or Jackson Pollock or Frank O'Hara, and I still kept an eye out for Mr de Kooning even though he wasn't really dead yet. Where is everybody?

Suddenly, I heard a mower in the distance, followed the sound behind me, turned around to see a man mowing the brown grass on the back hill where Hannah was. Is. The Steve Ross part. I shouted for him to stop. The Green River groundskeeper, I liked to think of him as the gravedigger like in *Hamlet* – "Alas poor Yorick I knew him . . ." He shut off the motor and stood there watching me as I slogged back down the hill. I wondered if he lived in the house with the dogs. It was good to see the man with the mower, alive and not sad. He was smiling. He looked like a man's man so I asked him where Pollock's grave was. In love with Pollock's big drippy paintings ever since I was a kid, I even remembered the titles – "Lavender Mist," "The Deep," "Blue Poles." I couldn't really remember what they looked like but I remembered what they felt like.

You may wonder what a girl from Great Neck was doing falling in love with Willem de Kooning's and Jackson Pollock's paintings at the age of thirteen.

"That's awfully young," Iris had said.

I think I was in love with Action Painting because there was no action music, no music with a beat and words my mother couldn't get. Can you imagine being a ten-year-old without rock and roll? That is if you didn't count "Slaughter on Tenth Avenue." I counted it. So much so that when the Poetry Project asked me to read at an event called "Epiphany Albums, the Record that Changed Your Life" that's what popped into my mind, an instinctive, embarrassingly ancient choice. Thinking about it made me feel like dancing. Then it made me feel like crying: a little girl and my father yelling at me because he came into the house when I was playing some music he thought was trash, playing it loud and dancing to it, bumping and grinding to "Slaughter on Tenth Avenue" and he glared at me and shut off the stereo, it wasn't even a stereo yet, it was a Magnavox blond console, though we did have the first components in our town, but that was a few years later.

"What is that crap?" he growled, like I was shit.

"But Daddy," I said, "it's a ballet. You can dance to it."

"You call that dancing?"

*

The gravedigger took off his cap and pointed right up the hill, in between Hannah and Elaine, actually.

"Jackson," he said, his finger still out.

He called him "Jackson." Unbelievable! Like he was an old friend. Very old, I thought. And it wasn't a gravestone. It was a real stone. It was a boulder, a big tan flecked boulder, I'd walked right past many times. So big it immediately made you think how much male sweat and testosterone must have gone into getting it there, unless it was already there. I didn't think so. There was a story about it I thought I'd heard. That Jackson used to piss on some boulders behind his house on Springs-Fireplace Road. I wondered if this were one of those. But they were supposed to be smaller. Check.

The gravedigger and I walked up the hill to where he'd pointed. The big rock had a brass plate on it with "Jackson Pollock" scrawled on it like he did, though I heard he had a problem with signing his work on the bottoms of his master-pieces. Slate flagstones made a little terrace. The gravedigger told me that before the new part was added Jackson's stone was at the top of the hill and behind was just low woods. I pictured that kind of messy mesh that was so common out in Springs, that made it a winter bird sanctuary. All those vines and berries – protection, wild and tangled – made me think it must have looked like a living Jackson Pollock painting. Or maybe that's what gave him the idea for the drips. So originally Jackson's boulder had sat on top of the hill, looking much bigger, with only the woods descending down behind it. Now that they've been cleared, the new part sloped back and down to the gravel road and the parking spots, making the stone disappear more. Maybe Steve Ross wanted the run-off from Jackson's grave to water his flowers.

Then out of the corner of my eye I saw another stone, a smaller yellow boulder. It's so odd the way now you see 'em now you don't, how things popped out at you the moment you weren't looking, where you'd been looking forever. This stone too had been invisible before, hiding behind Jackson's, a miniature version of Jackson's, about six feet in front of it. We walked on a few steps and looked down at the brass name plate with the signature on it, at Jackson's foot or feet? Was it Frank O'Hara? I'd heard that.

No, it wasn't Frank. The smaller boulder placed there belonged, of course, to Lee Krasner. It said "Lee Krasner," in script, too. Then "Lee Krasner Pollock" in type, below. Her plate was like his but scaled down. Way down. On the slate in front there was a bunch of little stones. I looked back at Jackson's. Now I was calling him Jackson. I saw there were mementos on his, too. A paintbrush and other objects. A whiskey bottle. But no little stones. What's with the stones?

"Here's Lee," I said, adopting his style.

"Yep."

But I was excited. Another woman. A friend for Elaine. Maybe I should get Iris to superimpose their gravestones, make them side by side. Isn't "Side by Side" a old song about friendship?

So where was Frank? I felt too embarrassed to ask. But why? Because he was gay? Because the gravedigger might not have heard of him because he's a poet? But that is his job. To know. No. Maybe I wanted to find him myself, like I discovered Elaine.

"Thank you," I said to the gravedigger.

He stood there with me a moment longer, then went back to work.

Poor Jackson. I wondered if Ruth whatsername, the pretty girlfriend of Pollock's who wrote that book about her and Jackson, was here. Was she dead? No. She's still alive, living on West 14th St in Franz Kline's loft. She'd be great to talk to. A friend of mine knew her, wanted to make a movie about Pollock from Ruth's book. Maybe she could introduce me. She was the one who didn't die in the horrendous accident that killed Jackson and her friend somewhere on Springs-Fireplace Road. Ruth's best friend Emily something came along so it wouldn't look bad for Ruth and Jackson to be out on a Saturday night. Emily died. Jackson died.

Ruth was pretty. I'd heard that Jackson used to joke about how ugly Lee was and what it was like being hitched to such an ugly woman. Did he deserve to die? For saying that? Ruth Kligman was her name, the surviving girl, an old woman now, I supposed. I should call her.

Each time I visited Green River, I found another mid-century art-world star: Harold Rosenberg, one of the two critics, along with Clement Greenberg (not here?) who championed the whole big Abstract Expressionist game. Which one wrote *Tradition of the New*? Who named it "Action Painting"? Check on that. Harold's stone was huge, covered with some Hebrew which looked scrawled on, like graffiti, like an afterthought. Funny. I never thought of these guys – or girls – artists ever – as Jewish.

As I wandered I realized that the signature of the cemetery, I guess because there are so many painters here, was signatures. Flamboyant names familiar from being seen scrawled across the bottom right of so many canvases I'd seen in galleries and museums were carved here in stone. There were a number I'd never heard of but which were scrawled with as much machismo as if they all had carved their big names one last time, though Ad Reinhart, famous for his square black paintings, had a horizontal white rectangular marble stone with his name carved in print. Simple, beautiful, the white rectangle was completely opposite to the painting he did in life.

One day when I was standing at Elaine's grave, fascinated by this big ugly green blob on her great big heavy stone, I noticed – how could I have missed it – this huge black gleaming monolith, the height of a tall human, with the signature Stuart Davis across it. This time I had one of those throwaway cameras with me, and I shot him. It was so buffed there was no way of getting "his" image without getting yours back at you in the frame, like it was your grave too. It gave me chills – and warm feelings too: back when he was still a nobody my Aunt Rita had bought some Stuart Davis paintings in the fifties for $3,000 a piece and hung them in their hallway in Kings Point out on Long Island. They were just the kind of paintings a teenage suburban girl in love with the City would go for. I did. Jaunty, spicy, primary color, tilted, literal, lyrical, flat, with words in them. Bouncy, with a beat, like music. (Last year Stuart Davis had a big retrospective at the Met. Then Rita died. My cousin inherited the Stuart Davis paintings, one of which sold for $350,000 at Parke Bernet. She bought a house in Truro with it, one designed by a Japanese architect.) When he died he was out of fashion. I was proud to have loved him then while he was still a bargain.

I kept looking. I found Jean Stafford, who was married to A. J. Liebling. They were lying next to each other, now forever, matching stones. Upright, black, matte. Nice print. Only the painters seemed to have script. Still, where was Frank? As my memories stirred about Action Jackson, Frank came alive again for me too. I wanted him. One of the first poets who became an art critic in New York. Was this true? I guessed the Americans were modelling themselves on the Europeans here, the Surrealists, Dada, an art–poetry movement. In fact the connection was more explicit: art and real estate. Many of the European Surrealist painters, especially Max Ernst and his wife Dorothea Tanning, came to East Hampton too. They were all friends. Someone, maybe Rothko, said the Surrealists gave better parties than the Abstract Expressionists. Perhaps the American Action Painters inherited some of their misogyny from the French. O'Hara gave the art–poetry thing an American twist, got a curatorial job at the Modern.

Then finally, one dark day, I found him. I literally stumbled onto him. He wasn't really near anyone else famous, he was under a bush. Poor Frank: the picture of him stumbling drunk on the beach in Fire Island, being run over by a dune buggy. Frank's stone was white and flat, lying down flat, like Ad

Reinhart. He was also carved like Ad, print, no signature, with a beautiful quote from one of his poems. I was as moved as the first day at Hannah's. Maybe it's the words: "Grace to be born and live as variously as possible."

# *Grace*

Grace. Was this the connection? To the Green River girls? To girls again? The next time I was in the city a strange coincidence occurred. Someone discarded, in a pile on the street in front of my loft, a book Elaine had written. It took my breath away. It was almost the same feeling as when I discovered her in Green River. Only this time there were pictures. Pages of pictures. In one of the two introductions a woman named June Silver told a story that hit me hard. It was about being a young painter who came to the city in the forties from the sticks and how she was in the Village one day and saw coming toward her, bopping down Eighth Street, two gorgeous girls, two women artists, talking, animated, brilliant, beautiful, the whole image of everything she'd dreamed she'd become part of: being talented and famous and most of all, famous friends. It was Lee and Elaine. I could see them coming, too, and that image got stuck in my head, permanently, like friends I'd bopped down Eighth Street with myself, as a kid in the fifties, before it was all shoe stores.

I looked at the photos. Elaine did remind me of Hannah

Wilke. She was pretty like that. I didn't read the essays Elaine wrote about art and other artists. I looked in the index for Lee's name. To my surprise it wasn't there. The book fell open to one page in particular. Top Pin Up Boys. First off I was mad. Why not girls on your list, Elaine. The era, I supposed. Then I was blown away. One of them was Grace's father. I couldn't believe it. Someone I knew was on Elaine's list.

Grace's father, Pindar Pelitin, though not buried in Green River Cemetery, and neither strictly Abstract, or Expressionist, was one of the boys. In "The Club" whatever that meant. I heard people say it but still didn't know if it was a metaphor or a place. I'd check. He was not an American, so he got lumped with de Kooning as a European, but he was a wilder blend, a Moroccan Jew who grew up in Cairo then lived in Rome until he met Grace's mother, an Episcopalian aristocrat from Cleveland who worked for an Italian radio station in New York. He had this mane of hair which made him even more intimidating to me. He was very respected because he got to be in the famous show called "15 Americans at the Modern." Big stuff. The year? Check. Big stuff because American modern painters were then something new. There had been big Americans, but they were realists mostly. So being in that show was big. Here was that whole beginning happening; the culture center axis shifting off Paris and London to New York, and to a lesser extent San Francisco.

Grace had a lot of trouble getting along with her father, whom she adored. Her mother, Lucy, did not participate that much in the art scene. Not unusual for the wives not to be there, except for Lee and Elaine, not because they were also considered and respected as painters in their own right but because both were their husbands' career handlers, I think. Lucy did no such thing. Grace would have, but she was only fourteen. Maybe if mother and daughter had, Pelitin would have been more famous. Everybody calls him "Pelitin" like he had no first name. Even his wife, even Grace.

Grace was my first love, my one and only real girlfriend. We were barely fourteen. She was big, sophisticated. She went to Music and Art. She lived in the Village. Her father was a famous New York School painter. Her mother had a girlfriend. We went to Off-Broadway shows. We went to art shows. I fell in love. With it all. Especially the art shows.

I imagine we're at Lee Krasner's solo show, her second. It's at Stable Gallery. We're the only kids there. The year is 1955 and the other new thing about Action Painting is New York. Not even the Greenwich Village of my parents' generation, but East Tenth Street, though it is not called the East Village. It's just low-rent nowhere. Pollock and de Kooning showed there. Grace's father showed there, and took us there to openings . . .

. . ."Oh my God," I'm tugging on Grace's long black sleeve. I'm speechless, almost. "They're beautiful."

There they are. I'm not looking at the paintings. It's Elaine de Kooning and Willem. He blond, sharp, delicate, strong, slender, his whole face and body like it was carved, made of material, not flesh and blood. But it's the woman standing next to him who takes my heart away. She's a beauty, so pretty, delicate and chiselled like him, but a bit softer, American, Brooklyn born though I don't know this yet, feminine, jazzy light sparking off her. Elaine has bangs. I have bangs. I reach up and touch them tentatively, then tenderly. It makes me proud. Secure. Elaine turns toward the door. There she is, the star of the show. Another woman, not so pretty, not pretty at all. But beautiful, strong, stylish, not dressed bohemian, black dress, below the knee, stockings, heels, fitting clothes, like something from a store you wouldn't have heard of, maybe from thrift shops. The bull next to Lee is, of course, Pollock. The waves parted for him, even though it's her show. She's wearing gloves. No, would she? To her own opening? An artist? She mightn't. Forget the gloves. I wonder. Did I get the gloves from a photo I saw of her wearing a little hat and gloves, but maybe that was taken at their house on Fireplace Road which had no heat.

What about the paintings? What do they look like? No wait, they're not paintings. It's coming into focus. They're collages. I can't catch my breath. I look at Grace. She's laughing at me. I'm such a girl, such a suburban girl. But she smiles at me, very deep and grown-up and happy to be taking me there, here, watching me find first-time excitement. Did I think the work was better than Jackson's? That's the catch. Because of who they are, Elaine and Lee, Pollock's wife, de Kooning's wife, it's hard to see their accomplishment clearly. If you say that the women did it first and the men just copied them then you feel stupid because the men are such incredible painters. That's it. They are in shadow, their work blurred because everyone thinks of them as the wives, though later I hear that Elaine when asked what it is like to work in de Kooning's shadow, says I never worked in his shadow, I worked in his light. Pollock is my hero, but I keep watching Elaine, moving around, flirting, drinking. She looks at us. She comes over to us. I clutch at Gracie again.

"And whose little girl are you?" Elaine says.

It's a joke. Grace is huge, not little at all. She is taller than Elaine.

"No wait, I know," she says. "You're Pelitin's kid, right?"

Grace smiles back and booms, in her thrilling low grown-up voice, "and you're de Kooning's wife!"

Did we laugh at that joke?

Elaine shakes both our hands. I wish she'd introduce me to Willem, but she just raises her glass first to Grace and then to me. But before she goes away she says, "You have nice legs, kid."

I don't. Hers are nicer, perfect, slim. I hate my legs. My calves are too big.

"You do," Grace says.

I remembered other things: bringing my best friend Joy in

from high-school one day to visit Grace. Joy and I'd been friends since seventh grade. Her mother died in ninth. It was so terrible. Afterwards, she practically moved in with my family for a while. I remember one night when my father, who was watching Nixon on our new TV, said in disgust, "If he's president, we're moving to Canada. And you, Joy, can move with us." Later she told me how much it moved her. It seemed important to introduce my best friend to my – what did I call her, not my girlfriend – but it also seemed more important to keep them separate, until one day I finally got brave and brought Joy into the city with me to meet Grace and our musical comedy teacher from summer music camp. My two worlds were colliding. I wondered if Joy could tell something was going on between me and Grace, or just assumed that Grace was a take charge kind of gal, maybe because she was from the city. Grace actually lived in Greenwich Village. Danny was the name of the musical comedy teacher. We went in Saturday afternoon. Joy met me after my art class at the Modern, which I took every Saturday morning. I had a crush on the pretty young woman artist who taught the class. I made a collage out of hot pink net I probably still have in my storage bin. Joy and I took the E to West Fourth Street and met Grace. I remember all of us walking, turning left onto Christopher Street, seeing the Theater DeLys, *Three Penny Opera* on the marquis, a blast of silver river. He played musical comedy songs on the piano. It made us homesick for the Cape. It was only later (in the afternoon? in life?) that we realized we were in a gay bar.

Sometimes I'd stay over at Grace's, sleeping in her single bed, though there was another bed in the room. We'd have sex. I remember her parents being home, being quiet, even though her mother had a girlfriend too. After my mother found and burned the letters Grace wrote to me, she (my mother) asked – nothing was ever forbidden in our progressive home – me not to see Grace again. I promised I wouldn't. Then I sneaked off into the city. Then my mother relented, somehow convinced, probably by all my convincing lies, that Grace and I were simply friends again and she let her come and stay at our house in Vermont. Grace brought her flute, and played it in the road, which charmed my father. This lasted until Grace went off to college, got kicked out from Bennington yet, for having a girl in her room, and then got sent to Rome. Throughout, we wrote. Letters. More letters.

That Labor Day weekend in Vermont, six months ago, when I stayed with Grace and her girlfriend and Paul and James and felt like I wanted to be with a woman again, something else happened. Grace told me she saved all these letters. The thought made me slightly ill for some reason. But her eyes gleamed so when she told me that I couldn't resist agreeing to take a look at them. She wouldn't let me have the originals. That they were precious to her made me iller. The thought of having to read them in her presence seemed potentially fatal. So I agreed to meet her at a xerox store near my loft to make copies. In the time we had to wait for the copies I told her that when I was at her house in Vermont with her and her girlfriend and Paul and James I'd woken up alone thinking I wanted to be gay too. I had to tell someone. I had to tell someone I knew well. I had to tell a woman. I thought I had to tell a lesbian. My mistake was telling Grace. She thought I meant her.

I stammered an explanation, an apology, clarification, but she was visibly hurt, angry, disappointed, humiliated. But she covered. She was always a great actress. And she still wanted me to have the letters – we were still waiting for copies. But really, how could anyone nurture a crush for thirty years without the least encouragement?

The point was it had nothing to do with her anymore. The point was I didn't want her, or anyone I'd wanted before. Throwing away my comfortable old life for new passion was the new point. Passion period. Even though it seemed completely unlikely that I would ever find my way, what I told her that day in the xerox store, my mentioning it to someone, made it more real. I wanted something. Something new. But then for Grace, her passion for me had never grown old.

# Cemetery of Signs

My visits to Green River had a rhythm. Each time, after Hannah, I would visit Lee and Elaine. I still knew nothing about their connection in life, but they must have been connected. They must have been friends. There was a group, a "community" then, New York in the forties and fifties, people who lived nearby, downtown, cold-water lofts, summers in P-town, East Hampton, all went to the same coffee shops, Rikers Cafeteria on Eighth Street and Sixth Avenue, the same bars, mostly "the bar," the Cedar on Eighth and University, members of "the Club." Whatever that was.

I even went to some of these places myself when I came into the city from the suburbs when I was in high-school. But the people had all moved out here by then. Probably I'd just missed them. I imagined they must have gone to the same parties and openings. Lee and Elaine must have been, especially early on, friends and colleagues, both painters, probably rivals, too, since their husbands were and they were both so behind their husbands. So far behind.

So Lee and Elaine, who like Hannah, never got the attention

from the world they wanted when they were alive, each time I visited, got it from me.

# Baby

One of Iris's pictures of Hannah didn't come out right. She needed to reshoot it. She insisted on coming back for a second visit. The next morning we went to Green River for a little while but by the time we got back to the house, though we were hungry, the kitchen was a mess of dirty dishes from last night and more than that, cemeteries, like I said before, always made me hot.

I nixed the cuffs, though. I liked the stainless steel, the clicking sound of them closing bit by bit, tick tick tick. But I didn't like the looks of the key. It didn't look like a key. It was just a little bent piece of metal and though I tried it on my own wrist a few times and it worked, the thought of being handcuffed to the bedposts in this yellow house scared me, even if the people who owned it edited radical books. I felt a little bit old for this, but we went with the scarves. Iris had a bunch of scarves she'd stolen from an old lady she worked for who, like so many women of her generation, had a huge collection of scarves they never wore anymore. Iris pulled them out one by one like magic, bad magic, cheap magic, coming out of her sleeve, her hat, her mouth.

"Lie down," she said.

"What are you gonna do?"

"I'm gonna tie you up, baby."

Since Iris was my student, her wanting to tie me up was a reversal. Good, I thought, to flip the power. The power switch. I was so tired of the way things were.

"Don't you want me to?"

I knew, even as Iris picked a blue scarf and a leopard one and waved them up for me to approve, that classroom teaching would never be the same.

"Yes."

"Lie down."

Iris tied my arms and legs to the bed posts. I was still in my jumpsuit, but Iris didn't undress me or say take it off like I thought and hoped she would. It was a one piece leopard-print sweatshirt-type material. It had snaps. Iris just began to unsnap it. Pop pop pop. I felt so good, tied to the bed, without choice, chosen, legs and arms spread; I hovered above myself, seeing my fantasy of the student's experienced fingers opening the teacher's clothes, unsnapping teacher, spreading her, sliding inside the material, over her breasts, around her shoulders, down to her navel over her belly and down into her bush, which was not as bushy, of course, as it had been when she was a student herself, much to her sorrow. I returned to my body and gazed up at the face on top of me, close, intent, the curly gray hair getting curlier from dampness. I started to thrash.

"Your chest is bright pink, baby. Why are you so red? Are you feeling something?" said Iris, a nasty tone in her voice, a taunting reference to my old Lucky Strike confession that if she ever came out, if we ever had sex, that I wouldn't feel anything.

"Talk to me. Tell me what you want."

She sounded hostile. She was not playing.

I wish I'd thought to say, Gag me, baby. There were plenty of extra scarves. But I kept my mouth shut. Frozen again. What was I supposed to do? A moment ago it had felt too good to talk.

"You gotta tell me what you want."

I still didn't get it. I felt like a baby. What was wrong with me? I wasn't much of a talker, never could think of a thing to say unless I had a funny story to tell. My style was so anecdotal. I couldn't think well on my feet, or, evidently, on my back.

"Talk to me."

I tried to think B-movie. "Oh, baby," I said, feeling like a fool. I forced myself by imagining Iris was forcing me.

"It feels good."

"Good what? What feels good, baby?"

"Uh," I was whispering, "to be tied up?"

"What? I can't hear you."

"It feels good to let you."

"Let me what, baby?"

"I don't know . . ."

"Tell me, baby."

"Explore me."

But funny how when I said it I felt a rush of lust. Iris had been right, as usual. It made a difference. Words. Then my head was rocking from side to side, my body pulling on the scarves, pulling the knots tighter and tighter. I felt so spread. Then suddenly Iris stopped.

"What? Why are you stopping?" I whimpered, could hear a little catch in my own voice between gasps.

Iris didn't answer me. She tugged at the last snap. It wasn't a real snap. It didn't really open. It was welded shut and then I realized that because of where the snaps stopped Iris could not really get a good feel any farther down without undressing me completely, and of course she couldn't get my arms out of my sleeves because they were tied to the bedposts.

It was so ridiculous. I'd assumed that Iris, though a student, would be able to teach me about the really important things

I'd missed in twenty years of tame monogamy. I assumed, from how she dressed, from her paintings, her writings, her carriage, and how she talked about herself and her girlfriends that Iris was experienced, had a clear and kinky and interesting sexual agenda. But things were going wrong again.

Like with the massage oil. After Iris left, I'd pulled off the little Henry Moore plastic bottle and tried to scrub the stain off, but it stayed. And why did Iris tie me up without undressing me first? I was beginning to get annoyed, not a sexy feeling.

Iris stood up. She bolted from the room.

"Where are you going?"

"I'll be right back."

Lying there tied to the bed alone was not a turn on.

"I'm not going anywhere."

I listened to Iris opening and shutting drawers, imagining pots and pans, once neatly stacked, being toppled and strewn.

"What are you looking for?"

"Scissors."

I felt scared. Pleasantly.

"Come back."

Iris opened the last closed cabinet. Was it the one with the bottle with the bit of booze in the bottom?

"Damn. I can't find the scissors," Iris muttered loud enough for me to hear her.

A better fantasy! I thought. Maybe Iris could just rip my clothes off even though the jumpsuit was from Bettina Reidel. My well felt like it was starting to fill up again with the thought. But Iris returned without scissors, and with a faraway glassy look. She went down to the bottom of the bed and loomed over me, scowling.

"I'm gonna have to untie you."

All the air went out of my balloon. The whole heated scenario deflated, taking my desire with it. This was not it at all. Iris started to untie one of the scarves.

"No, no," I cried, for the first time really expressing feelings.

"No what?"

"Don't untie me. Please." I was almost crying, but not quite. "Don't."

But I couldn't bring myself to tell Iris to rip my clothes right off me and leave me tied up. I tried to say what I wanted, like she'd wanted before, but the words wouldn't come. I was mad she couldn't figure it out.

"No. Don't."

"Yes. I want to put my mouth on you. I can't reach."

The knot was really tight from when I'd strained against the scarves, in an almost frenzy; it seemed like hours ago. Where was that lust now? Iris finally got the knot loose and slipped one arm out of the jumpsuit. At first it wouldn't come but by shifting me into a really awkward and, I was sure, very unflattering position, she wrestled the arm out of the jumpsuit and tried to go down but it still wasn't loose enough so she untied one of the leg scarves, too.

I was feeling something now: disappointment. Nonetheless I tried. I closed my eyes and spread my legs open very wide, trying to pretend they were still tied to the bed. Then I opened my arms wide and grabbed on the bedposts and tried to hang on and pretend I couldn't move. Iris knelt over me and began to move her tongue around. One of my hands was still knotted to the four-poster bed. It felt good to pull against it and then it just felt good period, first there and then all over. I pushed up against Iris, my free hand on back of Iris's neck, then backed off. I breathed into it. I waited, concentrated, stopped concentrating, let go. I felt like I had, at last, without trying, told all my secrets.

Iris was on her knees. Then she rolled over onto the bed. I was all spread out, head to one side, eyes closed. After a while I opened them and looked at her.

"Now you," I said.

"Wait a minute. I want to tie you back up first," Iris said.

First I kicked and then Iris helped pull the jumpsuit from the remaining arm and leg, and left me naked at last. Then she tied me back up. Tight.

"I'll be right back."

Iris came back into the room with her regular Polaroid. It flashed. I got anxious. Iris disappeared again.

"Where are you going?" I said, pretending to be exasperated, but really I was still purring too much to care. I twisted my head and caught a glimpse of Iris hurrying down the hall disappearing into the kitchen. She was fully dressed. I lay there, wondering about it all, half listening to Elaine, I mean Iris, thrashing about in the other room. It made me laugh. She was so ridiculous sometimes. I wiggled my toes, like a baby. They pushed up against the footboard of the wooden four-poster that was the prize auction item, the pride of Alex's downstairs decorating scheme, her latest, most costly acquisition.

I laughed. Loud enough for Iris to hear.

"What?"

I didn't want Iris to think I was making fun of her for trying to fuck me while I was tied up without undressing me first. She was very sensitive about criticism.

"What are you doing?"

"I'll be right there."

She sounded possessed, but not by lust. Maybe she was looking for the bottle of booze. I'd hid it. She'd never find it. I was pleased. I'd felt. I'd gotten wet. I'd come. I wondered if my happiness had something to do with my corny s/m fantasy not going so smoothly, that there were kinks in the kink that had to be worked out, hitches in the knots that had to be undone by the two of us together. Plus my Bettina Reidel jumpsuit was still in one piece.

"Oops!" Iris said. It sounded like she banged her head on the open cabinet door. Then she dropped a glass.

"Are you all right?" I called. I was beginning to feel something different, helplessness, even panic as I imagined that the kitchen now like the rest of the house. Thank goodness Alex would not be back for months. I'd have plenty of time to clean, maybe even have the floor by the bed resanded. Get a maid. The works.

"Oh no!" Iris croaked. "Oh my God! What's that?"

It sounded like the words got stuck in her throat.

"What's wrong?"

"I don't know."

She was sort of gurgling. I wondered if she'd found the vodka I'd hid.

"What?"

"It's a car," Iris choked.

My pulse rate went up too. Had she been in the process of swallowing too big a swig when she saw something? Someone?

"What kind?"

"I don't know."

"Shit."

"Big. Something in the driveway. It wasn't there the last time I looked."

"What if it's a realtor?"

"Shit."

"They're supposed to call," I said.

"I didn't even see it pull in. I was thinking about you." She sounded slurry, maybe just scared.

"Are you drinking?" I couldn't keep the rage of accusation out of my voice. How had she gotten me into this mess?

"Just a little. I almost dropped the bottle."

She was trying to make a joke, but I had no humor or sympathy. I was furious and scared. I pictured it shattered and vodka and chips of glass falling all over her and the sink and the floor and the room reeking. I wondered how long the car had been sitting there.

Iris raced down the hall to the bedroom where she'd left me tightly retied to the bedposts, yelling.

"It's people. They're getting out. There's someone here," Iris said. She did not sound cool anymore, almost begging, like she needed me to tell her what to do.

"Go see who they are," I commanded, faintly. I already knew what was coming.

Iris raced back out of the room.

"Look out the window and tell me from there. Don't leave the window. Stay near the front door."

"Three people getting out of the car, a silver-haired very butch woman from the driver's side and two very unbutch men getting out of the back seat wearing identical cable knit cashmeres and loafers."

"Loafers? What kind?"

"Oh, God. I don't know. They're looking at the house."

Iris raced back into the bedroom.

"I told you to stay out there."

"I don't know who they are. She looks like a dyke. Maybe it's just her haircut. Her hair's the color of her car," she shrieked as she disappeared again.

Now I was sure it was the realtor.

"You locked the door?" I called out, unsure.

Iris whirled back down the hall.

"Didn't you?"

Too late. I could hear the front door opening. I felt like I was going into shock. In my mind I saw the the haircut woman peeking in, waving "her" key.

"Hellllloooo!" she called in a chipper crisp voice. "Are we interrupting something? I'm Sandy Cross, from Pony Realty. I'm showing the house. Mr and Mrs Germaine said I could come anytime, I didn't know anyone was here." She was starting to race, having an inkling that it was not a good time, perhaps. Perhaps she'd gotten a look at the debris strewn all over the house and sensed that she was not going to close any deals. Still they'd driven all that way in from the city.

"Aren't you supposed to call or something," said Iris said in a loud voice, trying to match Pony Girl's assertive tone.

I'd explained the drill about showing the house to her one time in the car.

"Well, we tried," said Ms Pony Express, "but there was no answer."

I remembered we'd unplugged the answering machine when we came back from the cemetery, remembered how it scared me to do it, but I felt brave and excited. But I did not want Jack to call, to hear his sweet voice leaving a recorded message.

I could hear Iris babbling now.

"Well, you see, I mean, my friend, the person who's subletting the house, I'm just visiting, is sick and we just didn't get a chance to clean up and, I mean, maybe you'd better come back . . ."

I called out. This was my cue, but I wondered if she could hear me. The door was open a fraction which, when I realized it, scared me more.

"Iris . . ."

"Excuse me," said Iris. I could tell by her voice she was moving away from the front door and coming back to me. Don't leave them alone, I thought. I don't pray. My voice was silent but sharp, picturing the mystery threesome peering into the kitchen, the broken glass still on the floor, the dishes piled in the sink, the drain choked with artichoke leaves.

"Watch the glass," Iris called back over her shoulder as she ran out of the room, down the hall and slipped back through the crack in the bedroom door. I was flailing as much as the restraints would let me.

"Iris, for God's sake, untie me."

She began to struggle with the knotted scarves. She had tied them really good this time, planning to have a second go at me now that I was naked. The knots held.

We heard the agent calling her. Iris dashed back out, slamming the door. It sounded funny to me. Sometimes it didn't catch. I heard the second click as it unlocked and opened a crack again. At least I could hear her, hear them, coming. How would that help? I heard her run back in to where the woman and the two men were. I could tell they were standing in the middle of the kitchen.

"Is there a dishwasher?"

"No, but why don't you look upstairs first, the upstairs is beautiful, it's just been added, there's a balcony and a skylight." Iris was doing a pretty good job, I thought. I didn't know if I could do better. Still, I was scared, straining to hear, pulling on the scarves. Doesn't old silk tear?

"I'll tidy up," Iris muttered to the woman with the beautiful haircut. I wondered if she got it done out here or in the city. It sounded like Iris was trying to pretend that she and this woman were in cahoots, that she walked in on people whose houses looked like this all the time with clients who just drove three hours from the city.

"Send them upstairs," Iris said.

Good girl, I thought.

The upstairs was the one room we hadn't yet had sex in and so it was still neat.

"Later," said the agent. She liked to be in control too. At least on the job.

"Isn't there this cute downstairs bedroom?" the agent asked. "Come," she said to the men, who hadn't said a word yet. I pictured them glued to the floor, probably a combination of something we'd spilled and their own disgust, not moving anywhere near the stairs where Iris was trying to steer them or in the direction, toward me, that the agent was pushing. They liked to be in control, too. It was their money. I was grateful for that.

"It's fabulous. I remember that room from last summer," the agent babbled on.

I could hear her voice getting closer.

"Great for guests. Can we see it?" she said to Iris. "It has the most wonderful four-poster bed," she cooed to the boys.

"No," Iris yelped, then tried to bring her voice down an octave. "I mean, not really, not now, that's where my friend is, she's not well, like I said, that's why it's really not a good time, we didn't even have a chance to straighten up or do the dishes, as you can see. The doctor just left," she improvised. I could see her pushing a strand of hair behind her ear, a habit she had, which would look good now, like she could do a bit of light housekeeping on herself.

"Well, we'll just take a peek. Come."

I heard them start to walk down the hall, heard a shuffle of feet, almost felt the silent struggle as Iris must've stepped out to block the hallway, trying to distract them with the one piece of good art in the house.

"That's a real Sue Coe."

"The bed is to die for," the real estate agent said.

"She might be contagious," Iris shouted. "The doctor said—"

Did they hear a howl from behind the not-quite-closed bedroom door, the four-poster creaking and groaning? I couldn't help myself. The sound slipped out. I was ready to pass out. I heard Iris lurch again, throwing herself in the agent's path, then pulling the door shut and standing against it. I heard it click shut, muffling the hushed sound of leather soles twirling on the shiny hall floors as they turned back, walked, heels clicking away down the hall, and took another look around the bare living room. It had almost no furniture, just a stereo, a chair, a Duraflame log, a TV and a filthy flokati rug.

"Very Shaker," the realtor said, a last pitch to the men. But they were already out the door.

"Bye," Iris waved.

I pictured the agent, wiggling her fingers, Iris wiggling back. I knew she'd never done that in her whole life.

I heard the car doors. That dead sound really good cars make. Then I heard Iris lock the door. My whole body was already locked up, still tied hand and foot with her silk scarves to the bedposts. It was too late to laugh. I heard her walking back toward the bedroom. First she stood in the doorway. Then she moved down to the foot of the bed where I could see her. Her eyes were glazed. We weren't really looking at each other at all. I was frozen, terrified, sunk. Why did this feel so personal, like I was undesirable? The way the men spun on the heels of their fucking Gucci loafers and waltzed out the door? Like they didn't like the house.

# Missing

The next morning we went back to Green River. What happened would have been funny if it hadn't been so awful. I was taking Iris on the full tour I always took myself. The ground was hard and bare. We walked up the hill. After revisiting Hannah I showed her Jackson and Lee. She shot them. I pointed out Stuart Davis. He had his picture taken. Ad Reinhart, Frank O'Hara.

We were walking along, the snow crunching, chatting, we got up the hill and turned and gasped. No big hideous pink and verdigris stone, no name, no date, no nothing. Just a patch of pebbles that might've always been there. I couldn't believe it. Elaine was missing.

# *Blur*

How could she do this to me? How could a stone of such monumental bulk get up and walk away? I remembered my own grave/cradle-robbing experience, an incident I hadn't thought of for a long time. When Stefan and I ran off – at least he wasn't my student, he was my second husband's student, a French–Polish Adonis psychopath, who knew how to rant, a European Abbie Hoffman – we'd left my spouse tripping his brains out on a subway platform, the West 4th Street stop.

I may have had a severely altered lifestyle, but it was 1969 and I was caught between generations, in the crossfire between youth culture and Cosmo culture. Since every other grown-up couple had one, Stefan and I had a contract, too. Ours had nothing to do with money or chores, though: our deal was no matter what, 1) to stay together for a year, 2) not to lie to each other (to facilitate this there was a clause that if either of us went away we would leave the reel-to-reel tape recorder running), and 3) to try something sexual we'd never done before the night the Americans landed on the moon. And we kept all the agreements, except the last. We never got it together to have anal sex during the moonwalk. We were too busy trying to cop.

We were in Vermont, my very first summer in Grace's beautiful old farmhouse. She'd offered it to me for free when Stefan and I ran off. She'd never approved of any of my husbands. Her father had died and she'd called, after years of silence, to invite me to the funeral. Though I bailed at the last minute, we'd seen each other a few times after and were in one of our closer periods.

I can still smell the barn in the heat. I was addicted to speed and hence addicted to snooping. I was in the perfect place. I spent time poring through boxes of her father's art supplies, which she'd taken there after his death. All the pretty colored pencils. I sifted through bundles of letters she kept in the spare room, imagining somehow I'd find the ones I wrote when we were teenagers, to even out my mother's having found hers. Little did I know that even at this point I was looking in the wrong place, that Grace had saved all my old letters, not in some dilapidated farmhouse she never visited but in her office in the theater district, already filed by date and sealed in plastic.

After the summer Stefan and I moved to a nearby college town. I'd gotten a teaching job late in August. It was another time my life was changed by an obituary. I remember being at the lake, reading the *New York Times*, miserable about the prospect of having to return to the city when the cold set in, even though my new love was already taking an old toll. I happened on an obit, the page I always turned to first, of a man who taught, by the most amazing coincidence, at a little local college in the next town. I'd met some of the students over the summer, doing drug deals. It was a low-key place, a school for kids who had already gotten kicked out of four other schools but were too scared of their parents to drop out. The dead man was head of the English Department. The term was starting in two weeks. I had a PhD. I drove over that afternoon and had a contract a week later.

By now that contract and the one Stefan and I had was

about to expire. Now, after the momentous spring of Cambodia and Kent State, almost a year after the moon landing, it was early June. We rented a gatehouse to a big estate which had its own private cemetery, and it was now time to pack. We had trashed the house. All hell was about to break loose. All we spoke about and did was drugs. We were burnt, totally. One day in the car we had the ultimate argument.

"Maybe we should stop," I said.

The car screeched over to the side of the road and I bumped up against the dash with a thud. We'd been doing 80 mph.

"I didn't mean the car," I said.

"I know what you meant," he said. "Why do you want to stop?"

"To have a baby," I murmured. It was not true, but I had to say something that sounded corny, sane.

"Shit," he said. "You couldn't stay straight for nine months if your life depended on it."

I'd come back from an anti-war protest in D.C. one weekend and made myself listen to him whispering to some sixteen-year-old he had picked up in White River Junction.

"Your ass is so soft," he whispered.

"Mmmm . . ."

"It's like a baby's."

I remember the feeling of listening, like I was listening not with my ears but with my guts, which were being pounded by every word, by sounds that were not words. The tape was hissing. I had to keep on, keep it on. Not because it was part of the contract, but to prove I was free.

Stefan had stopped off in New York to see his Polish mother. When he came back, he found me inside the house with two students, a boy and a girl, from my sixteenth-century lit. course. All the doors and windows were locked. When he looked in we were all just making the bed. But he ran from door to door, window to window, rattling and shaking everything, and when I finally let him in he was so furious that he made me strip, pulled the phone out and kept me that way for almost a week so the only way I could meet one of them for one last time was to slip a message via the other who visited one day: come to the cemetery at 11, and I somehow escaped. The student had rowed all the way across the lake in the pitch dark to fuck me. We met in the cemetery and got down on this little stone – on the grave of a baby. The kid moved too fast, like someone more used to jerking off than fucking. It was then I swore off students.

Of course Stefan had caught me and we had another screamer of a fight and didn't speak for another week. But then we made up around our leave-taking. By our last night in Vermont we were fine. Except that I was speeding so I wanted to take everything with me, the old furniture in the barn, the beautiful carpets in the big house, plants from the garden. But I settled on this one thing and now I was tiptoeing out of the house and up the noisy gravel drive to get the little headstone I'd seen in the little cemetery. I was making Super 8 movies at the time, and I wanted to use it as a prop.

The whole gravestone was no more than a foot tall. It was the newest stone in the cemetery, only eighty years old. It was made of plain polished local granite. The head was crowned with three scallops, alternately small large small, then arcing in a graceful curve before coming down small large small on the other side. Below that the capital letters were simply carved and highly polished: BABY. What a great movie title shot for a romance, I'd thought. Love and death: BABY.

I squatted down; my hands closed over the stone cold slab. Something seemed to stab me in the stomach. I tried to lift the headstone out of the ground, tensing my muscles. It came right off the long iron post it was just loosely sitting on. The post was an inch in diameter. It fit into a hole drilled six or seven inches up into the center of the stone. It slipped right off. I was so surprised I almost fell on my back but its weight thrust me forward. I stood there resting it on my thighs and then started to run with it.

Just then I felt something go inside me, go heavy and cold

as the stone itself. My stomach knotted and twisted. The anxiety was unbearable. It wouldn't have surprised me if the night clouds parted and lightning struck.

So I turned back. I was still bent over, not from the weight of the headstone but from the convulsion of fear a moment ago. Try as I might to get it back on the rusted spike, my hands and thighs were trembling too much. Why was it so much harder getting it back on than getting it off? Finally, hardly breathing or even feeling my agony anymore, I crept from the little cemetery. I made sure the gate didn't make a sound as it closed, then ran for the safety of the house, the warmth of the dark bed, his dark sleeping body. But he was waiting up for me.

"Where were you?" he hissed. "Sneaking out for one last fuck?"

"Yes," I'd lied.

But Elaine was not a baby when she died in 1989. Her stone was much too heavy for anyone, on any kind of drug, to lift. I was still in shock. It was all my fault for cheating on Jack. I hadn't expected change, retribution, to come so fast, to hit me so hard. Or maybe it was true that if you take a picture of someone you steal their souls? So take a picture of a gravestone – wrong in the first place, and the stone would disappear. That might explain it. It would also make it Iris's fault. I hadn't asked her to take that first shot of Elaine's stone, that old rusty brown Polaroid, with the antique 4×5 camera she borrowed from school when she came out to visit the first time.

On the bright side, at least we had proof.

"What about the Polaroid you took last time?" I said. "If Elaine never comes back at least we have a picture of what used to be here. We have the evidence."

She whipped out her camera, took another shot of the grave, now just dirt covered with small round worn multicolored stones and pebbles – I still thought the pebbles were a Green River tradition, like the little stones on Lee Krasner's grave.

We stuck a red tulip we stole from some local man's fresh grave for color.

"It's here. It's here," she said. "The picture. It's in my journal. In the car."

I couldn't believe she had it with her. We dashed back to the car. But when we took out the print, the scariest thing yet was happening. The original Polaroid image was disappearing; a hole was growing in it, a doomy white area in one corner that looked like a cloud, or something taking a big bite out of the rest of the picture. Elaine was missing there too.

Maybe it had to do with exposure to light. Iris shouldn't have been carrying Elaine around with her. But I couldn't help thinking it was more than that. I was confused. I'd been so filled with satisfaction about the sex, how far I'd come, how hard she'd made me come, how happy I'd been when it'd happened. Now, everything was fuzzy. I felt like the old Polaroid. There was hardly any image left. All that was left was a big white hole. A big blur.

It reminded me of that photograph of me and Francis before the prom that Hannah's sister gave me after the funeral. Now it fit. Maybe Francie's and Elaine's blurred images were somewhere above us, floating away, dancing. Or making a movie about Green River Cemetery. About Elaine and Lee.

Maybe someone took Elaine away because there was something I didn't know about Willem that the locals knew, about his imminent demise. I'd heard that Willem was still painting brilliantly even though he had Alzheimer's and couldn't remember painting anything. Maybe he was dying and they were making a new stone. I couldn't quite picture either of these strong types allowing themselves to be conjoined under one headstone. Would it say, like the title of the bio – I still hadn't read it, or even found it, in which everyone says Elaine comes off like such a sexual shark – "Elaine and Bill"?

What if Elaine had actually risen from her grave once the stone was gone? What if it wasn't even missing? What if she had pushed it off, the opposite of the story I'd heard about how Jackson's stone got to his grave, how Lee made a bunch of guys excavate it from the woods near the house and lift it and haul it, the incredible weight almost killing two of them, it getting put down by inches with winches and chains but in the wrong spot and having to be hauled all over again, all on her orders. But if Lee could do that, maybe Elaine could move her own stone away, maybe disappear it, as a rebel gets disappeared.

What if Iris had been right about Elaine after all? What if Elaine sneaked off, up out of the ground, or underground, and slithered over to where Hannah Wilke was, the prettiest girl in Green River, and that's why the mound of earth on Hannah looked so stirred up the first time I saw it?

Elaine had come back to life, was now, now that her stone no longer held her down, alive again, a ghost, given a second chance. Maybe, after Elaine got Hannah, the two of them wiggled their way over, underground, and got Lee and freed her too. Then maybe Lee and Elaine finally got to be together at last. Not just friends but lovers. There was so much publicity when that Elaine and Bill book came out and showed Elaine in a bad light, some thought, though her sexual aggressiveness seemed okay to me. What if Elaine and Lee ran off? In all the books about Lee Krasner and Elaine de Kooning, none of which I'd read, there was nothing, of course, about that. But maybe after all those years of being married to those big macho art star men, when they do come back as ghosts, they come back as lesbians. Maybe that book – you could call it *Elaine and Lee* – hasn't been written. Yet.

# *Friends*

Where are we now? Lee wondered. The Springs General Store? Jackson had traded a painting for food in the early days. We used to bump into each other here, all the time.

Elaine bumped into Lee now.

"Oops."

"What are we going to do? We have no money."

"Do we need to eat?"

"I don't know, but I can still want to. Right now I want ice cream."

She'd taken a pint of Heath Bar Crunch and slipped it under her . . .her skin. What are we wearing? she wondered.

"I don't understand any of this," Lee said.

"Did you ever?" Elaine said.

"You were always smarter than me."

"Lee. How could you say that. You were vanguard."

"Thanks."

"More than any of us. More than Jackson. Before him. He was lucky to've met you. Without you, he'd be nothing."

"Thanks."

"That's not what I meant. I meant, was there ever anything to understand?"

"You were so good with words. Still are."

"I was just a better flirt than you. Maybe," she said, kind of jaunty, almost like she was flirting with her now, "this time around, we will."

"Will what?"

Lee was nervous, especially about the theft.

"If you're so smart tell me, are we walking? It just feels like first we're one place and then the next, just moments of being here or there."

"Didn't it always?"

"Will what?"

Lee and Elaine walked right past the counter. The owner's son was leaning on it, talking to another customer – the postman. Lee recognized him. So did Elaine. They hid.

"What if someone recognizes us?" Lee whispered.

"There's no one here."

"But what about that one, the one getting cookies?"

"Does she look familiar?"

"All women of a certain age look alike."

"How old do you think she is?"

"She looks angry."

"I wonder what she's thinking about."

"Shhh," Elaine said and slid the Häagen-Dazs down the counter.

"This yours?"

"No," said the postman.

"Just leave it. I'll put it back," said the man behind the counter. While he was bagging, Elaine slipped it away again, and they slipped out the door.

"Possibly they can't see us."

Lee felt so sad.

"At least we won't have to worry about not being recognized."

"Were we ever?"

They laughed.

"We've had a lot of practice."

Their eyes were tearing.

"Did we ever worry?"

"Yes," they both said at once. Lee felt like collapsing on the floor. It was fun. She hadn't had such a good time in years, she wasn't sure why. It was nice to be with Elaine and not feel all the things they always felt – the tension, the competition, the jealousy. That was a big relief, and she said so. Or did she just think it and did Elaine pick it up?

"Maybe this time that will be different, too," Lee said.

"You're getting smarter by the moment," Elaine said, winking, if you could call it that.

The woman who'd been in the store came stomping out in the snow and got in a red car. Elaine and Lee were quiet. She slammed the door.

Time passed. A minute. A week. A month. A year? They found themselves at the door of a yellow house in the woods near the bay, at the corner of Squaw Road and Babes Lane. Then they found themselves inside. The funny house was empty, except it smelled like fire. It was a beautiful smell, so familiar, the lingering smell of an old fire in a cold house.

"Very Shaker," Elaine said.

"What do you think happened? I mean what the hell is happening, Elaine?" Lee said.

"I wish I had my notebook," Elaine said. She jumped up and ran out of the room, from room to room. Lee heard her yelp with joy.

"There's a computer."

Lee could hear the little whir of power, the beep, the click of keys.

"Elaine," she said, getting up reluctantly. The fire was so warm and she was so cold. She came into the room in the end of the hall where Elaine was at the screen. Lee stood behind her. Elaine lunged forward. She didn't want Lee to see.

"Go back to the fire. I'll be there soon."

Lee did what Elaine said. This was a first.

She listened to the fire.

Elaine called, "Do you know today's date?"

"You're putting me on!" Lee laughed. She hadn't used that expression in a while. Wait. She saw a newspaper near the hearth, waiting to start a fire. She grabbed it, looked at the date. Was it old? It was yellowed.

She stood up and brought it in to Elaine. The hall was narrow. There was a lithograph. Lee looked close. She liked it. Sue Coe. Yes. She'd heard of her, maybe. But when she came into her room – she already thought of it as Elaine's room – she blinked hard. The room was painted a bright yellow, covered with posters she didn't think much of. In fact, the house had no taste. No artists lived here. Lee held up the paper. Elaine moved her away with her arm.

"But you wanted to know the date," Lee said. She hoped she didn't sound whiney. "It's the *Star*."

"The *East Hampton Star*?"

She kept typing, little ticking finger touches, speeding, even when Lee shoved the paper in front of her. She looked at the date and gasped.

"I can't believe I've been dead four years."

"For years."

She kept on writing. "I felt the earth move over my head . . ." The words kept coming out.

Lee left. She understood the creative process. She'd been leaving artists alone all her life, been alone. She heard the printer.

Elaine came back in.

"Let me see."

"No." Elaine hid it.

"Please."

"I can't show it."

"You've known me fifty years."

"If the *Star* is right."

A silence.

"Read it to me."

"It's awful," Elaine said. "I've forgotten how to write. If you don't write every day, you lose it."

"Did you really write every day?"

"Almost. Then when I got my computer I went back and started transcribing all the early stuff."

"Someone should publish it."

"Oh God! What if they do! All those names! I guess it doesn't matter now. Or . . .does it?"

"Look," Lee said, showing her what she'd found in the paper. "Hannah Wilke. Remember her? And what a beautiful drawing. I don't ever remember seeing them reproduce a drawing on an obituary page, do you?"

"She wasn't even that famous."

Elaine frowned. The print was small.

"She was only fifty. Too young."

"No such thing."

"Yes. To die."

"What's upstairs?"

"It looks newer."

"You're very smart about houses."

"We all were."

"They were all so cheap."

"Not my new one."

"I wonder if you can see the water."

Lee went up the new stairs first. She could feel Elaine looking at her ass. For the first time in years she wasn't self-conscious. Everyone always said she had a great body but in the end her ass got big.

"What did you mean, Elaine?" Lee said.

"What when?"

"Before, in the store, about not being recognized before. That that could change now. Now that – now that what?"

Elaine opened the Heath Bar Crunch. Holding out the spoon

to Lee, she said "—maybe that can change. Maybe we can change that, now that we are—"

Elaine pulled the spoon back a little, making Lee strain forward to reach for it, which she did,

"—now that we are—"

Elaine wondered what it would be like to have sex with Lee.

"Now that we are—"

Lee wondered how she was going to finish the sentence. Now that we are "alive?" "Dead?"

"What?"

"—friends."

# *Palm Sunday*

The next day I woke up with two tons of cement on my chest. Maybe when Elaine had been liberated when her stone disappeared they used it to bury me. I had two kinds of work I loved, teaching and writing. I had two lovers, of two genders. I had two cats. I had two houses. City and country. Soho and Springs. Each $350 a month. I should have felt twice blessed. But I felt doubly cursed. A two-timing double-crossing bitch. Buried.

After I got back to the city, I feared being caught by everyone. School was now a nightmare. When a memo arrived in my mailbox, reminding the faculty of the consequences of inappropriate behavior with students as well as a reminder that there was no smoking in the classrooms or hallways, I freaked. But that wasn't the only thing. The class was already spoiled, as I knew it would be. My anxiety about what I was doing wrong, my fear that she had told, my self-consciousness cramped my improvisational style. It made me stiff. I tried but suspected I was failing to treat Iris like a regular student. It ruined it for me, for everyone.

Iris was there talking to her younger friends when I walked in. She looked up, smiled in a nearly neutral way, even though her hand pointed down to a large 18×24 Kodak yellow cardboard envelope stuck behind her chair, which she left when class was over, disappearing with her friends. Usually she hung around. The others had stopped waiting for her, leaving her with me. But this time she'd walked out too. All that was left was the big envelope in the empty quiet classroom. It seemed risky to open it here but I couldn't wait to look. There's one of Frank, the text clear and sharp, and the masterpiece, a new one of Elaine without her stone, all blown up, beautiful, the stolen red tulip tilted to one side in the pebbles the shape of a body. But I was furious at Iris for bringing me the new photos. I knew people would ask her where she took them and when and how she got out there. Would she tell? Sleeping with teacher? What a prize. Could she not? I was in knots.

The lying was killing me. At home I hid my collection of photos of Elaine – the brown Polaroid Iris had taken the first weekend with the big white hole in it (I convinced her to give it to me even though there was nothing to see), the new one with the red tulip. I kept taking them out and looking, the one without the stone was so clear, so final. The one with the stone was disappearing.

The next night Iris called to see if I wanted to go to the Joel-Peter Witkin show with her. Jack answered the phone. Afterwards we had a fight again about me letting my students call me at home, especially at night.

"I'll get my own line."

"That's not the point."

She called again. I could have killed her. He glared. My stomach ground, but I agreed to meet her on Saturday on Fifty-seventh Street. It was the first time we'd seen each other in the city, outside of class. I didn't want to be seen with her. I was afraid someone who knew me and Jack would spot me with Iris. Tell Jack. Her pushiness pulled me two ways, got me angry and excited. I had sworn that I would never spend time with her in the city. But that resolve crumbled fast. I couldn't say no.

At the gallery they had reprints of this article about Joel-Peter Witkin. After I got back downtown I read it over, glad to be home but unable to completely detach from her either. It wasn't the photos so much, at least not his photos. There was one of him, his wife, another woman, and a couple of dogs. The caption said he had a wife who had a girlfriend. It grabbed my attention. It occurred to me that maybe I could get this two thing to work. That I wouldn't have to break my old life apart, but could merge the old and the new, like Chichi, a six-foot Amazon I spent some time with on the beach in Truro, who had taken lots of estrogen (too much) so s/he had amazing tits but insisted on leaving his big dark Columbian dick, because, as s/he said, I'm into addition, not subtraction. Chicchi had a lot of problems but at the moment, s/he seemed like a good role model. As good as Joel-Peter Witkin's setup. The big advantage would be that I could be open about it. There'd be photos of the three of us, like Joel, his wife, her girlfriend, a dog. Maybe we'd get a dog. But this part was a problem. The cats might object to this new arrangement more than Jack would. I looked at the magazine pictures again, the ones of the wife, lover, and husband, and thought it could be me. I resolved to speak.

But the next day was Palm Sunday, our twentieth anniversary. I now know, from an Oprah show, that you're not supposed to use holiday celebrations to drop any bombs, like when the whole family gathers for Thanksgiving is not the time to tell your daughter she's really adopted. But it seemed like such a good idea at the time.

Twenty years. Felt like half my life. We had champagne and pancakes for breakfast, and a high conversation in which he made the toast.

"Twenty more, don't be a bore."

We touched glasses. I gulped, but saw my first opening. You don't want boring, I thought? I was so determined not to let this day pass without bringing up the Joel–Peter Witkin idea. Probably the champagne.

"Can you imagine twenty more," I said, almost whispering, my stomach knotted way up in between my chest and my throat, I felt like gagging, "without . . ." voice trailing off, lost resolve . . .

"What? You're mumbling."

"Can you imagine," I cleared my throat, "a whole life of no sex with another person?"

"I don't think you have to worry about that for me," Jack said. "I'm not thinking about it. Maybe if I were on the road, surrounded by a lot of other women or something."

"Well," I said, thinking of the Beatles song, "maybe when I'm sixty-four," I said, "I'll have a girlfriend."

"Eh," he said.

I tried to pursue the conversation, which definitely seemed to take a lot of prodding. We did not have conversations like this. Never did. About "us," about sex.

"Well," I said, "I think at this point our relationship could survive our having sex with other people."

"Well," he said, "in the beginning of a relationship it would be terrible, but I guess it could happen later."

But he was not enthusiastic about it as a concept, I could tell. I was about to bring up this couple we knew and how many lovers they'd had and even threesomes with their lovers (once, many years ago before Jack, a threesome with me).

"Did you really never have sex with anyone since we've been together?"

"Well," he said, "except for X—"

I heard her name and felt a crushing instant of wild nervous jealousy. Oh, no, I thought, what have I started? I'm going to have to tell him about the rock star and the oral sex with the poet which left me with a condition, like tennis elbow. It lasted years. I called it blowjob elbow (but only to myself). I pictured scenes in bad movies and books where everyone spills out all their affairs and much crying and accusation – at least we were not in a restaurant – and then making up and tears and resolution and fabulous sex. I always thought he'd been carrying on with her all those times I went out of town with my mother during our early years right after my father died. I'd call, say from a booth on Prince Edward Island up in Canada. He'd say "Oh, I'm just on my way out to brunch with X and her friends." I'd get lightheaded and nervous. I'd get off the phone. My mother would say is everything all right, knowing I was having a green jealousy fit, but I'd lie and say yes. She'd know anyway, which had been a comfort. Now my heart raced in the same way at the thought of having this conversation.

"Just that one time," he said, "on Bleecker Street—"

I was amazed. Relief flooded me—

"—and that was before we moved in here so that doesn't really count, does it?"

"No," I shook my head, "it doesn't because we weren't living together," even though it was in my bed in my apartment, and I did get that migraine in the middle of saying the word "jealous."

It was when I came home from seeing my parents in Connecticut. I knew he was seeing her because she was going to Vancouver forever the next day, and they'd been a couple back in high-school. I asked him if they had sex and he said yes and I said that's okay, I'm not "jea" – and I was struck dumb with this full-blown migraine, the only one I ever had, right between syllables – "lous." It didn't go away for three days, and I had to spend the entire weekend we'd planned in Montauk in the motel room with the shades down and the Watergate hearings on the TV, the picture dimmed way down, John Erlichman's voice and my migraine, forever linked.

I felt good that this one time with X was all. But I was also thinking, Uh-oh, waiting for it to be my turn. But he didn't ask me. He didn't say, what about you? Instead he poured more champagne.

"This is the best day of my life," he said.

I gulped. The day went on. I was still feeling somewhat wonderful from Iris, though I could tell I was starting to feel a little sick from a cold coming on. And I still felt like I'd like this imagined conversation to have a little more shape, a bit more resolution, though I could see I wasn't getting anywhere.

Then we went out to dinner – our favorite Village restaurant – though it was too cold to sit outside and my stomach was now totally upset. He made the same toast.

"Twenty more, don't be a bore."

He suggested we celebrate in another twenty.

"Well, by that time maybe you'll have a boyfriend and I'll have a girlfriend," I said, realizing that I was being pushy with my agenda.

"Forget it," he said. "I won't have a boyfriend." He shook his head in an attractive way, "But I know you want a girl-friend," and he smiled slyly—

—gulp—

"—so have one."

# *The Net*

He'd given me my opening, but I closed up. The next day she showed up at the loft. I couldn't believe it. By chance, it was Sunday, Jack was not home. She couldn't not have known that every Sunday, since we'd known each other, he went to visit his mother. Moms, as we called her, was great, lively, singing and dancing when we were there, playing cards when Aunt Rose came over, but getting lonelier and more forgetful by the minute and Jack was starting to panic, so he'd stay later and later. Since my mother died I sometimes went with him. But not this Sunday. I wanted to be home alone. I was never in the loft alone anymore. So I was pissed at Iris, partly for spoiling that, and furious that she was putting me in such a dangerous position.

We were, by sheer coincidence, both wearing our sheer net bird bras. The first weekend she'd come out, one of the amusements I'd devised to stay out of serious trouble was to go underwear shopping. We'd gone into a very fancy store in East Hampton, all frills and hearts and bows because Valentine's Day was coming. Iris stomped in in her boots and looked out of place but acted completely at home. The young women behind the counter had looked at us as if we were about to take off the whole store. So I'd bought her a bra that was black sheer with little birds over the center, the birds more opaque. The birds weren't all that little. Nipple vultures. It was quite an effect. I'd bought one for each of us. They'd cost $90 dollars.

Iris took hers off. She made me keep mine on. Hers lay on the floor right beside the mattress. One of our recently adopted cats, Josefina, came over. We'd gotten a family, a mother, and two six-month-old kittens. The two females, mother, named Mamasan, and daughter, Josefina, were torties, the boy, Stuart, an orange tabby. He'd dropped dead in the middle of the night last year, when he was only fourteen months. Sudden Infant Death Syndrome, or some kind of congenital heart failure. It was three a.m. on Sunday morning. We'd heard a crash. Then a thud. We dashed downstairs from the sleeping loft. Stuart was lying on his side, eyes open a little, maybe breathing. Josefina was sitting near, her eyes wide, her hair on her back and on her tail standing straight up.

I tried to blow into his mouth but nothing happened.

"He's dead," Jack had said.

But Stuart's big orange kitten paws were soft and warm for hours, as I held them. His eyes were still open. Finally I took a pill and slept with him downstairs. It was awful. I'd always wondered what Josefina saw. Her eyes were so wide. I felt like I'd been hit by a truck. We were left with the girls, mother and daughter.

Josefina started rolling around in Iris's bra. She pawed it, sniffing it, got all tangled up. It must have been very sweaty, a special kind of sweat because she was going ecstatic just as I was. It was funny except for a moment I imagined this cat having a heart attack too. Saw her rolling wildly around in the cups of Iris's black net bra, eyes wide, like when Stuart died. It made me nervous. Afraid for what Josefina was seeing now:

that somehow, she'd give me away. Afraid I'd have to run screaming, naked, hysterical down to call the vet and out onto the street with a dead cat in my cat box, looking for an angry cab on a Saturday afternoon on Soho when the traffic was barely moving, to see if the vet could jump start her heart. And while she was at it, mine. If she died on me now, I'd really be fucked.

# *Shades*

I went back to Green River as soon as I could, by myself. The gravedigger, Mr Barnes, was there again. I was glad to see him, like he was my only local friend. I told him that Elaine's stone was missing. Funny, he hadn't even noticed. He said he'd ask the head of the Green River Association about it.

Now I was expecting there'd be buzz all over town. I bought the *Star* to see if there was a story about it. Nothing. I saw him a few days later, on my usual farewell turn en route back to the city. He said he hadn't had the time. He told me I should call this woman who ran the Green River Cemetery Association. She could be found under an awning company. I thought that was funny, to look for the head of a cemetery in the phone book under Awnings. Awnings and shades. You could think of death like an awning. Or a shady business. They could have little awnings over the graves, to protect the stones, or the flowers, to keep the snow and rain off. "Shades for Shades." I'd suggest it. The committee must have meetings.

What if I made a fuss and they pinned the whole thing on me? Or me and Iris. I liked having been seen with Iris around town. She always made a big impression wherever she went. She talked to strangers, asked odd questions, made direct contact. When we waltzed into the video store, the woman behind the counter seemed to assume we were a couple. I didn't know if she was a dyke, but I liked the feeling. In the country, on account of the haircuts and the pants, it's hard to tell. She didn't make us pay for the miniature Reese's peanut butter cups by the counter, so I wondered if that was a sign. I wanted everyone to think we were a couple. The gravedigger seemed to. When I came back without her he'd say where's your friend. But then I pictured our pictures in the *East Hampton Star*, or at least an item in the police blotter column about their suspicions. Someone we knew would see it, show it to Jack. He'd have to ask, wouldn't he? The relief I'd feel, having him find out by reading about it in the paper, having him find out without my having to tell. Or lie. It would get us talking.

I decided that if I went to this cemetery association meeting I'd go alone, I wouldn't bring Iris. I was afraid if we went in as a couple there would be talk, maybe resistance. I pictured old-timers, WASPS. There are lots of gay and lesbian people in the Hamptons of course but I doubted many of them would be on this local committee.

# *Polaroid*

There were other mysteries. I wondered about the little stones. Not only were there more on Lee's terrace, but mysteriously, since last time, a few had appeared near Hannah's little brass marker. I thought real Jews didn't put up proper gravestones for a year. My mother was so assimilated that she had Frank Campbell on the Upper East Side do my father. And when she died, I did her the same. So now their ashes were both sitting on a shelf somewhere in New Jersey. Not even next to each other. I couldn't visit. Since coming to Green River so much, I almost wished I could.

There were new smooth stones around Hannah's brass marker which was already there the first day I found her. Who put them there? Was someone else visiting Hannah regularly, besides me?

Another freak thing happened, to make me even more off balance. One morning I swung back over to Green River to see if Elaine had come back. As I walked up the hill my heart started slamming as I got nearer to her grave. It had warmed up some, but as I got closer, what was on the ground, as I got to Elaine, where snow'd been yesterday, made me start to shiver. There was a Polaroid, a modern one, not like the one Iris had taken with the antique 4×5. It was lying on the damp grass. It showed the stone, clear, the color of the green blob accurate, the date sharp, just like I remembered it before it disappeared.

Who took it? I could only think it must have been Iris. But when? I didn't see her. I was with her, drove her, every time she was at Green River. She didn't drive. She didn't have a car, didn't have money. But who else? How else?

I was convinced she'd taken the picture before we made the discovery together, lied about it, hid it, came out on her own and placed it on the grave under the snow. That look she gave me when I'd stalled her off about coming out again this weekend, muttered something about "next time," came back to me. I was afraid, now, really scared. Was she haunting me? Where was she? Was she out here now?

I drove back to the house. I didn't know what to do. So I called her. There was no answer. I kept calling, kept wondering where she was, expecting to find her hiding in some room in the house, or coming into my bedroom in the middle of the night. I didn't sleep at all. Maybe she was really crazy and my saying no had pushed the red button. Maybe she had committed suicide. My punishment was beginning. The thoughts I had – still ghosts of thoughts, about leaving home, leaving him, living alone, living period, were bad. Putting myself in danger from a deranged student who was stalking me was just desert for not telling him about her, or for telling her "next time," not really meaning it: I had invited disaster.

I got into the car. I needed to go back home. Maybe this time, when I got to the loft, I'd stay. Jack had this sweet habit. When I was in the middle of writing and I'd get up to pee, I'd come back to find I LOVE YOU on my screen. I remember the first time it happened it scared me. I didn't understand, thought it was coming from his terminal like they did in the movies, though I knew we weren't that hooked up.

Each time it happened – it had happened again, right before I left the last time – it still shocked me. These words, coming from nowhere: I had to erase them to keep going, but I felt like I was doing something cosmically wrong when I deleted. Now I longed to see them. I promised myself next time I'd just leave them, in the middle of whatever I was writing. I needed them now. Maybe this time they'd say I WILL ALWAYS LOVE YOU. He listened to the radio, too. Hell, he had a subscription to Billboard. He read the charts.

I thought about saying goodbye to Hannah, Lee, and Elaine maybe for the last time, and got as far as the Springs General Store and pulled off the road. I went in for coffee and another cookie. Soon, I'd be getting fat. I sat in the car and ate it. I thought about Iris again. Then, tired, tires screeching on the gravel, I put the car into reverse, backed out, made a U-turn and headed for home. I mean the city. Jack. The cats. I didn't need her, or Green River Cemetery or Elaine or Hannah or Lee or any ghosts. I was plenty spooked.

# *Mortal Thoughts*

But I couldn't leave it alone. The next time I came out I returned to Green River. Mr Barnes and I were still puzzling over Elaine's disappearance. It had been weeks now and no information. I bought the local papers, read the Police Blotters to see if vandalism had been reported, read the art columns, even the real estate sections. I almost got my nerve up to call the awning and shade lady and go to the meeting of the Green River Cemetery committee. But luckily a friend called and said she knew someone who was on the committee and I called her instead. I figured it'd be easier to drop in for coffee and ask this one person if she knew anything about Elaine's disappearance than to have to bring the whole question up before the committee and bring on suspicion: what was my interest? why was I so obsessed? So I called the Cemetery committee person and she said I could stop by. I could have asked her right then on the phone why Elaine was missing but I wanted to meet in person so I could tape. Maybe she would tell me other stuff about the cemetery.

She invited me in. We had some weird tea. We talked about

Green River, and Steve Ross's new part, the whole issue of expansion. The Hamptons were getting so crowded. There was no place to park. I made a joke that the problem was particularly critical when you were looking for that final parking place, but she didn't laugh. Unfortunately, she was a new member of the committee, and young, didn't really know much about the cemetery or artists in general. When I asked her about Elaine de Kooning for a second it seemed like she didn't know who I was talking about. I asked her about the missing stone. She had no idea. She said she would try to find out.

"Could you bring it up at the next meeting?"

"Well, we don't meet that frequently," she said. "I don't even know when the next meeting will be. You could call Mrs King."

The awning and shade lady, I almost said. I don't know why I was reluctant to. She gave me the number.

It still struck me as strange that you could just go in and take away someone's gravestone without anyone knowing about it. I asked her if she knew other women artists who I'd find there.

"What about Perle Fine?" she asked.

"Who?" I never heard of her but was embarrassed to say. I felt terrible.

"She was a painter."

"She's there?"

"Yes. Buried next to her husband, I forget his name. You know how they do. One headstone, two names. I didn't know them. They were neighbors of my mother's," she said.

For a second I wondered if she meant neighbors in the cemetery.

"I'll look," I said and turned off my tape recorder which had nothing useful on it and left.

It was snowing harder. I felt discouraged. When I left her house I turned the wrong way and at first there was no place to turn around. Finally I pulled into the school parking lot to make a "U" to turn back toward home, but either I didn't look right or did look but was dreaming and didn't see that this huge truck, an eighteen-wheeler with no business on this small populated street that must have been taking the same short cut as me, was barrelling down the hill. I was careening around the school parking lot, a big load of old snow shovelled to one side obscuring the sight lines; I pulled right out, almost right in front of him – thought it was a him – in the path. I hit the brakes. He hit the brakes. It was icy. I imagined, clear as ice, my brakes not holding or his not, me sliding in front of him. My hand shook. But I did stop and he did, in time, screeching, squealing, honking. I was so anxious I barely heard his curses, but I felt them. Felt cursed and lucky at the same time. Felt like Jackson Pollock smashed, getting smashed up on Springs-Fireplace Road, which was exactly where I was heading, passing the cemetery where he was buried after he went barrelling down the highway that night.

I pulled over after the near miss. My heart was still beating loud and fast, my hands gripped the still-cold steering wheel. I tried to breathe, wondering why it was so hard to be social after writing in isolation for days and did I really want to find out things about the people I was writing about? Did I want to know? Was there anything anyone could tell me? Were all the people I wanted to talk to, to ask if Lee and Elaine were really friends, dead? Or in Florida?

I drove home. The light was on in the dining room where I'd been working. I liked the way in the dark in the country, house lights fell out the window onto the snow and were gold. I couldn't see in from the car but inventoried, in my mind, as an exercise, the table: the bottle of Finlandia, the Schweppes seltzer, Body Shop apricot lip gloss, checkbook and unpaid bills, list from perfume shop for smell exercise, Uncle Leo ms., Toshiba 1850, Fez matches, half-smoked joint in brass Shiva ashtray my cousin the scholar brought back from India, miniature Phillips head screwdriver for doing little drug triangles, as opposed to lines, Zona Tranquility candle, *Mortal Thoughts* case, cassette in VCR, En Vogue case, cassette in box. Nine

Inch Nails CD jewel case, CD in box. First draft of sex scene, which was all I'd written so far. I'd written it as if it were happening to Lee and Elaine, not to me and Iris. I was into the idea of writing a ghost story. I went inside and tried to look at my print-out. I couldn't read it. I was so lonely. Was this what it's like to be dead?

# *Bead*

"I'll bring asparagus," she'd said when she'd called the next time.

It was supposed to rain all weekend. I tried to postpone for this reason, but she'd said the weather didn't affect her.

"You get wet in the rain, don't you?"

"You know how wet I get."

I got goosebumps. It would be the next "next time."

"What are you afraid of?"

I couldn't have said what I was afraid of so I said, "If I write about Lee and Elaine coming back as lesbians, they could sue me."

"They're dead."

"Their families."

"You love getting in trouble. Besides, maybe they'll never find out. Those people'll never read you."

That hurt. Made me nervous. Could I get sued? I'd have to remember to ask Bobby, who, being a big editor, would know. Why do I want to make Lee and Elaine come back as lesbians anyway? To make it funny? Funnier than the truth. Maybe it

· 110

was just a good one-liner. I'd only told it to Iris, who roared, and Bobby, who didn't.

"I'll talk to Bobby."

"Add it to your list," Iris said.

That night the sky turned purple. It wasn't so cold. Something was changing. Iris went out and took a picture of the color, with the black tangled treetops barely visible against it. I went out separately and saw it. I wanted to tramp through the snow to look for branches and small sticks to start the fire because we ran out of Duraflame. But there was no flashlight.

"Be careful."

The light from the house cast some shadows but not far enough. The bare bushes where the birds lived were like the treetops against the deep purple sky, interwoven, like tangled mesh stockings. It was pitch black. Like black Pollocks. I reached out in the dark into some terrible bush of thorns and got caught without knowing it and then made matters worse by ripping my hand away not at all gently, without trying first to extricate the thorn. Wanting to pull back from the pain, I instead took it with me. I ran inside, holding the throbbing finger up to the candlelight, and there was this dark red gob, globed, a big shiny bead, really huge, bulked up, already viscous like a big red bloody pearl, the size of a dime. Iris flicked on the overhead and held my finger. Her eyes went wide. Then she bent over my hand and started to suck greedily. I was shocked. She came up with blood on her lips and an expression in her eyes I'd never seen. Anywhere. She wiped them, her lips not her eyes, she wasn't crying, not yet.

"You taste like metal," she said, swallowing my blood.

"Metal?"

"Like iron."

She smacked her lips.

"Delicious," she murmured.

"Unsafe," I said.

I didn't mean to be mean. But I must have hit a big nerve. She was an activist, had brought ACT-UP safer sex posters into class. She lectured everyone about it. I pulled back my finger and I wagged it at her, like a kindergarten teacher. The blood still ran. This huge deep ripped cut had almost torn the whole tip off.

"Don't tell anyone," she pleaded. "Please don't ever tell."

I could hardly imagine saying to anyone, Oh, Iris sucked my blood the last time in East Hampton. But I got mad.

"I thought you said it was so important to tell the truth all the time."

I knew I was taunting her, because we'd fought before. Turned out she'd told her friends she was out here again and gave them the number. When they called I answered and got mad and said, "It's supposed to be," I couldn't say a secret – I couldn't even be honest about lying – "we're supposed to, uh, you promised to be discreet." She said, "well if someone asked me directly where I'm going to be this weekend, I cannot look them in the face and lie. I cannot do that to a friend."

I could not disagree. But I was seething. And frightened.

"If they want to be able to reach me, I have to tell them." She was a phone junkie.

Then she called some woman she was planning to meet on Sunday night.

"You've no right to be jealous of me," she said.

I slammed the door.

When I drove her to the train, I felt doomed. It was pouring.

"What's wrong?" I said to Iris. We were sitting at the station. The train was late. I was trying to make contact though I knew it was too late. I wanted her to go. We were pushing each other farther and farther away.

"Is it the weather? It's so depressing."

"Weather doesn't affect me," Iris said. She'd said it before. This time she sounded furious.

I looked out the window. I was trying to account for her dark mood, trying to change it.

"You know what? Last night, after you were asleep, I had this great idea," I said. "I forgot to tell you. To get someone to put together a show at Guild Hall called 'Lee and Elaine.' "

" 'Elaine and Lee,' " she said, grudgingly. She was cheering up.

"Whatever."

She looked grim again.

"No," I said, trying to repair again, "You could help me."

"How?"

"Your old teacher, wasn't she one of the Guerilla Girls? We could bring them back to life too!"

"I couldn't."

"We could sneak in one night."

"Was Hannah a Guerilla Girl?"

"I doubt it. She was a loner."

"Find out."

"We could call them Guerilla Ghosts."

I remembered a few years ago there was a Lee and Jackson show. It was called "Krasner–Pollock, a Working Relationship." Or maybe "Pollock–Krasner." But there was a lot of controversy about it, about implied influence, but I couldn't remember what the big deal was, but the Lee people weren't happy and the Jackson people were insulted, or something. I remember thinking finally she got represented in a big show and it was still in relation to Jackson and then people ended up saying snide things about her, like she was using him: it made Lee look bad after all she did for him. It was at Guild Hall. Lee was still alive. The show came to the city. I saw it. Everyone used it against Lee. A friend told me he went to see it with the poet Rene Ricard. It was still called "Pollock–Krasner, A Working Relationship." "Well," Rene said, "it's still working for her."

"Maybe we could," I said. I was excited again, had hope.

"You'll never do it," Iris said suddenly. It hurt. "I hate it when people don't do what they say."

She slammed her door as she got out.

"Wait."

"You never do anything you say you'll do. You'll never leave him. You'll never even tell him."

# *Blood*

The cut on my finger healed but left a big scar. Every time I thought of the amount of blood that poured out it threw me. Back to a memory that I'd buried, which got me closer to understanding what might be about to happen.

One night, after Jack and I got back from Vermont, right after school started but nothing had happened with Iris yet, I came home and walked into the kitchen. The house smelled funny. All the lights were on but it was empty. I walked into his studio. The door was open. The computer and the keyboards were still on but the music stands were toppled. There was blood on the walls, handprints and footprints and big drops all over. I retraced my steps and opened the door and called his name. I looked in the hallway and saw blood on the stairs. I called his name again and ran downstairs. The people in the furniture store came running to me.

"Thank God you're home."

"Where is he? What happened?"

"EMS just left."

"Where'd they go?"

"The VA hospital."

I looked around the store. It smelled funny too. There was blood on some of the expensive furniture and the carpets.

"What happened?"

They couldn't really tell me. He couldn't tell them. They all looked completely freaked and it wasn't only because of the blood all over the Beidemeirs. They implied that Jack was bleeding and hurt and incoherent, but he kept saying, Call 911. Call 911. So they did. The EMS workers came and were getting ready to take him to Bellevue, when he regained enough clarity to remember to say he's a Vietnam vet and still dripping blood and sweating, ran back upstairs and found the special form in one of the cubbyholes in his desk and came back down to the waiting paramedics. Then he said take me to the VA hospital, because he had no insurance and that way it'd be free. Then he fainted on the loading platform. The EMS people took him from there.

I ran out. Joe, the store boss, followed me and pointed down to the industrial steel loading platform, with that raised diamond pattern I always loved. It was covered with blood. Joe's accent was heavy but I got the point. I threw my arm at a cab that was zooming up from Broome Street.

"Wait," said Joe. "Did you lock your door?"

I felt crazy. Of course I'd left the house wide open. I ran back up and then came down. No cabs. I ran to the corner. I got one at Spring and Broome.

At the hospital they asked me who I was. I knew enough to lie and say his wife though I hated that. He was in ICU. I got scared. He looked terrified. He was hooked up to monitors. I'd heard hideous things about VA hospitals but here in ICU anyway, it seemed totally professional, spotless. Everyone was helpful and concerned.

"We don't know what the bleeding is from. We're testing him."

"Am I going to be all right?" Jack asked.

He was biting his cuticles, tormented.

I looked at the doctor. He tried to shrug reassuringly.

"You should take these home when you go." He handed me his pants.

Eventually they sedated him and I left.

"Do you have a plastic bag?"

The nurse brought one. I wrapped up the pants, bloody, shitty, sweaty, all the excretions of fear and disaster and dumped them in the nearest garbage can.

I visited twice a day.

They diagnosed it as a bleeding ulcer, probably caused by the Naprisin he'd been given after gum surgery. He was still afraid.

I went home to the empty loft each night and realized it was the first time I'd been in the loft for an extended period without him since he'd been on the road. It might have been ten years. When he was on the road, although I liked being alone, I wasn't writing yet and I was always insanely jealous. But this time I was writing and he was in the hospital. No dancers who invariably whipped off their clothes in front of him for all those quick changes in the wings.

Then I was the one going away. Taking trips to LA and now this venture of renting the house in Springs. I was glad. I mean I was sorry he was sick, and felt awful those first days when he was terrified. But even then I had a split funny double feeling. I flashed back to when I was very young, married for the first time, hating being married, feeling totally trapped. But the only way I could imagine getting out of the mess I'd made, the marriage ending, was him dying. I even fantasized the scene.

I am in Mexico. I am sitting in a café. His best friend shows up. I have a crush on the best friend.

"I have bad news."

My heart jumps in two directions.

"He's dead."

"Oh no."

The grieving widow. Mexico. The fabulous sex.

When that fantasy stopped working I even imagined me dying. Rather die than speak out?

I knew I was feeling that way now, only I didn't want anyone dead. Even back then I'd pulled myself together and got a Mexican divorce. My father had gone with me. After that I married another guy I wasn't in love with and took a lot of drugs and ran off and ended up fucking in the little cemetery and trying to steal the BABY stone. Then I met Jack and we moved into the loft. I'd lived with him for more than twenty years and knew that my feeling so free when he was in the hospital was a very bad sign.

# *Florent*

Could that have been only six months ago? October. It was April now. The second semester was more than half over. I couldn't wait to be done. It kept getting harder. Iris developed a swagger when she came into the room. One time she came right up to my desk. I hated her when she did that. But this time she leaned forward, put her lips close to my ear. I could feel myself blushing.

"They know!"

Then I recoiled.

"Who?"

I felt like I'd been hit.

"Probably everyone."

I couldn't read her face. Was she gleeful?

"What happened?"

"Lana."

Lana, another older student in the class, possibly vying for my attention, definitely presenting herself as hipper than thou, had been walking out of Florent shortly after Iris, Marta, and

I came in and sat down at the bar. We all said hello, but it was awkward.

"She saw us at Florent."

The night before class, Iris and I had gone out with her best friend, an ex-student of mine, to dinner. I knew it was a mistake. Iris and I had never gone out in public except for the Joel-Peter Witkin show. We had never been with anyone else before. We were both nervous, like we were admitting something, flaunting it. I knew Iris had told Marta about us. Marta'd been in my class the year before. She was the girl who actually told Iris to take me, take my class.

We ate at Florent, a French diner in the meat packing district.

"So?"

"She told everyone she saw us out together."

"How do you know?"

"Liz told me."

"Lana told Liz?"

"Liz told me Lana was telling everyone."

"But Marta was with us. There were three of us. We were just at the counter," I said pathetically. "Marta was in the middle."

I remembered purposely putting her there, but it was the corner so actually Iris and I had good eye contact. All three of us did. It felt good. Almost normal. But more exciting. There was a point where I did have my leg somehow wrapped around Iris's for a moment but I'm sure that was later. At least I hope it was Iris's.

"Well, she's telling everyone."

For a moment I wished it had been Jack or a friend of his who'd seen us so he'd know without me having to tell him, but the thought of all the students knowing, and then someone telling a teacher was worse.

I was furious at her.

"Did you have to tell me now, before class? Why didn't you wait till class was over? How'm I going to teach this class?"

The most awful moment came when, a few nights later, my phone rang: my boss.

"You're in trouble," she said. "The President wants to see you."

It'd happened before. She always ran interference for me, but this sounded serious.

"What about?"

"I don't know, dear, but you better call him."

"Now?"

"In the morning."

I was in trouble. I called. But it was only about a report he'd had about smoking and drinking in my classroom.

It had happened during the Erotic Aroma Unit. The idea was to bring in something you thought smelled erotic and to write about the journey you took to find it. The aromas floated into the hall. There were the usual vanilla candles, fresh cut lemons, a tee-shirt, a sweaty bra, leather smeared with KY and cum. Someone brought chocolate. I brought a black rubber sole. Some people brought the obvious – red wine, some fragrant herb. When the class was over, one student looked at me and said what're we gonna do with this wine?

"What about the herb?" Iris looked at me, daring me.

I wanted to just say no. I'd started to say no to the whole affair, though not to her. I didn't like being bossed. She was too demanding, especially about telling Jack. I already felt trapped in my own passivity. I wanted my freedom but I wasn't ready to make the break, and she was so intolerant of my waffling. She was pushing too hard, too soon. Now she was doing it again.

"Open the windows," I said and left the room. They lit up, poured wine into paper cups and had a party. The room reeked. But I didn't hear anything and forgot about it until someone in the alumni office next door said they thought they smelled pot. I denied it. It'd been a breezy day.

"I thought I smelled something too, Pete," I said to the President. "I'll keep my eyes out," I said. I knew he didn't

believe me, but he had no proof. Now I had two people to
break up with.

# *Pink*

I never understood Alex when she said she hated it when spring came. I thought it was just that that's when all the New Yorkers came back to the Hamptons. But it wasn't that. Springs was not traditionally just an artists' sanctuary. The area was also a bird sanctuary, nothing but fleets of trees in seas of vines for them to nest in. When there were no leaves on any of them the whole world was like handmade twittering lace. There were hardly any other human winter residents near the yellow house, so there were millions of birds, whole tribes of cardinals and blue jays and also squirrels, sparrows, crows. Ours, said Bobby, was the only lunch in town.

The winter was still, beautiful. Not empty, bleak or cold. It was a black and white world. It didn't change. Like the cemetery didn't change. I liked that. I loved that. I needed that desperately. At first I couldn't figure out why Elaine's stone disappearing upset me so much. Sure, I had already gotten attached to her, to her and Lee, some fantasy I had about them getting together, lovers, even more, being friends at last, free from the competitive vectors that buzzed around them in the art scene all their lives, even after their husbands were dead – oops – well, out of the picture, so to speak. Maybe there was competition between them because they couldn't openly compete with their husbands. I'd have to find out.

But it was more. The cemetery was the still world that was never supposed to change; in fact, you could count on it not to change. It was okay not to. Even best that way. That's what I'd liked about Green River. It was comforting, especially since, in the rest of my life, change seemed so dangerous, almost devastating to me – that if things changed I'd be left with nothing. So with the disappearance of Elaine's headstone, it seemed like nothing could stay in the same place anymore. It added to the pressure I felt from inside, not to mention what Iris kept putting on me. That's why I was on this mission to find out what happened. Maybe I needed to learn Elaine's secret. How she could be gone so easily, so fast, without a trace. Who gave her permission to leave?

Then spring came. I was more mixed up than ever. I could still hear Alex ranting about how horrible it was, saying how first there's this horrible yellow period and then everything is that bright young new green and then the worst of all, the pink. I found the most painful part wasn't the yellow and pink even, but before, the very first signs. Everything's still bare and muddy but things poke up, like little dicks, purple dicks, little yellow shoots and some bursting red sexual buds on things. It disgusted me and distracted me and I realized that things change and I was still stuck. I took a picture of Hannah's grave with clover all over it, looking like she was pushing it up, though that's daisies.

Then it went pink, mostly azaleas and rhododendron and laurel. And then, to my surprise, pink became my favorite color. There was a dogwood tree outside the house. In winter I'd hardly noticed it, a small, bare, crippled little tree standing between the male and female holly bushes. But the first time I came out in April it was dark pink red. It was unfolding. And change seemed beautiful again. Even possible. Elaine's stone was still missing, which depressed me, but there were fresh flowers on Lee's grave. I wondered who that admirer was. There were those little stones too. And more stones on Hannah's, and I wondered who put them there.

The next weekend the dogwood was lighter pink but still young and fresh, not quite open, a kind of perfection. Now I loved the spring. Bobby and I gave each other obsessive calls every time we traded off the house.

"Is the tree still pink?"

"Yes."

"Can't be."

"True."

It had been brilliantly sunny and softly, benignly mild since April 1 and now it was almost May. The thought that my lease was up Memorial Day was beginning to make me anxious, and I came out more and more. Each time our tree was out more and more too. It kept coming and staying pink. It was a miracle. I began to worship it. I was very worried about it changing into nothing. Droopy leaves. How tragic I would feel when the blossoms fell off. I wondered what would be left.

I asked Jack if he wanted to come see it. I don't know why he said no. So I called Iris, though we hadn't been in contact outside class.

Things had fallen apart, without our discussing the reasons. School was so hard I couldn't wait for it to be over. I couldn't stand sneaking around, couldn't bear to deceive Jack though I wanted to leave him. For the moment, it seemed easier to stop seeing her. But the one time she'd called me at home, she told me to come to her apartment and I couldn't refuse. I made up some stupid excuse to Jack and ran out the door, but when I got there all we did was argue about why I couldn't stay. I got up to leave.

"I have to go."

"No. You have to come."

She followed me down to the street. On the second landing she pushed me against the wall and slid her hand under my dress. I nearly fainted. I knew I was pink all over under my heavy clothes.

"Thank you," I said.

I bolted down the final flight of stairs and reached for the heavy front door too fast, somehow snagging this ring she gave me with a camelian (for courage, blood, heart) on the catch. I pulled. It held. My finger was crushed. The ring was bent. I tried to slip it off but it was too tight. She stuck her key in between the knob and my finger and twisted.

"Ow."

We finally got it off. It was no longer a circle. Not even close. It had a big dent inward which inversely matched the already swollen inside of my finger. I never should have worn it out. I mean on the street. I don't know how it got so bent. It must have been a cheap soft metal. My finger was bruising, already swelling, throbbing. I hurt.

"I'll fix it."

"Forget it."

"Let me."

I threw it at her.

"Goodbye."

But now, weeks later, I called. I invited her out for one last time. Fully dreading the encounter and fearing that all this sunshine and warm unseasonable heat would kill the blossoms on the pink dogwood, I knew she must see, and shoot this tree.

Then, the day before she was due, after six weeks of continuous balm and sunshine, the sky began to cloud up. The tree was still there, still pink, looking a bit fragile. It started to rain. I panicked. What if the rain tore all the final blossoms off and by the time she got here the tree would be empty? Worse, what if it just rained the whole time she was here? It would throw us together, lock us inside in a way we'd come to know was disaster. The second morning it was still raining and the blossoms held. I spent part of the morning scrambling around trying to rig a shelter out of shower curtain around the tree to protect the blossoms for that one day, but it fell down. Instead, I ran inside and went around the house sticking up photos taken during the good times with little rolls of tape, then abandoned all these projects as silly, perhaps humiliating, put them away. But when I went to take the pictures down the Scotch tape pulled patches of royal blue paint from the living room wall where they were. The walls, one of the other ways Alex had tried to spruce up the decor, now looked terrible.

I put the biggest picture back up, the beach, bright and blue, me in a light blue man's shirt, sun on my face, eyes closed but the rest of me smiling, in the wind. Behind me a snow fence undulated, bent back over from the heavy winter accumulations and storms, bleached almost the same color as the sand. Then I took that down.

En route to the train station to pick her up, I swung around past Green River Cemetery. The big Labs started to bark at me in that friendly way. Their tails swung damply in the rain. By now they knew me. I went as usual to Hannah first, but then as I walked up to see Lee and Jackson my blood started pumping hard in my throat. Something was very different. It wasn't just spring, the color, the buds, the green, the grass, lots of new bouquets and a few fresh graves. There it was. I couldn't breathe. I had no preparation. I'd seen no workers even though I was there the day before. There was no trace of disturbed earth or tool marks. No footprints. But there she was. Elaine was back.

I was confused. Where did that leave her? And Lee? And my ghost story? Did their affair peter out? Did they have to come back? Could they not stand not being dead? I looked hard at her stone. It looked the same. Or so I thought at the time. Then I started to feel happy in a way I hadn't because this would be something to give to Iris: a present, a secret. I still wanted to surprise her.

"Hello."

I couldn't wait to tell her, but she slouched off the train carrying her equipment, a big tripod bag, hunched over in her leather jacket and did not smile. It was pouring. We did not hug. Inside the car I said, "I've got a surprise for you."

"What?"

"It's a surprise."

"You know I don't like surprises."

"You'll like this one."

She guessed.

"What? Elaine's back?"

I was crushed. I should have stuck with my original scheme. I'd planned to swing round to Green River Cemetery on the way home, pretend I didn't know yet, and since we'd discovered her together, let Iris have the same racing shock I'd had, gasp, smile, light up, together, the return as mysterious as the disappearance, as marvelous. But I knew I couldn't fake it.

"I want to show you."

"I have to pee."

I tried to beat back my disappointment, tried hard to still think of it as a magnificent kind of closure since this would be our last weekend together and Elaine's stone had been missing since right after our first. But it was raining hard and she didn't care. So we didn't go there.

I couldn't believe the weather. What terrible luck. We were both very depressed. We rented three movies and bought ice cream, like the first time. One of the movies, which we watched in the afternoon before Iris got so drunk, was *The Rapture*. Nobody'd liked it much except me. I didn't really like the ending but we improved it by stopping it early, right after Mimi Rogers blows her little girl's head off and then puts the gun to her own throat but can't pull the trigger. They are in the desert, waiting for God. Just before she kills her daughter, Mimi asks, "Do you love God?"

"Yes, Mommy."

"Then tell God. Tell God that you love him."

There it was again.

"Talk to him. You have to talk to him. You have to tell him."

I'd stopped at the liquor store to buy some more vodka because Bobby had one more weekend in the house and we never left each other a dry house in case one arrived late in the night. But since it would be his last weekend too I was just going to get one of those small pint bottles. But something possessed me to get the liter and to get the 100 proof. That night, after I went to bed, Iris drank half of it.

When I woke up she was drunk and miserable. We watched some more movies, fought, I slammed a door, she drank some more. It was still raining. She managed to take some probably incredible pictures of the pink dogwood and then I drove her around town and she took these close-ups of the azalea parades, pink, white, maroon, purple, lavender, rose, cream, big bursts of color with little bits of green beginning to stick out in a sickly kind of way. Soon it would be all gone. It rained at night too, harder and harder. But the pink dogwood held. We were both drunk and fighting.

"Why are you so sad? Why do you look so sad?"

I remembered the same tone the first time we fucked when she said, why are you so pink?

"I'm not sad," I said defensively.

"I hate you! You're trying to hurt me!"

"I am not."

"You never see me or like me or appreciate me for what I am. You don't think I'm smart."

"How could you say that? You're ridiculous! Why do you always make everything so impossible?" I said.

"See. You do think I'm ridiculous!"

"That's not what I meant."

By ten o'clock she'd finished the bottle. I was still trying to keep up, just to keep her from poisoning herself further. At one point we ran outside. We stood under the pink tree and looked up through the blossoms into the black wet sky. She was holding the empty bottle. I took off my shirt. She looked at my body then tilted the bottle back and tried to get a last drop. I put on my shirt again.

"Why did you do that?"

"I was cold."

She was incoherent, still holding the bottle she'd finished hours ago. But she seemed furious. My stomach was in knots of fear and rage.

"You don't love me."

It seemed so out of the blue. We'd never spoken of love. Her expression changed. My anger started to go away. She looked so down.

"Let me help you up the stairs."

"Okay."

"I'll put you to bed."

"Yes."

I walked over to her and put my arm around her waist. She reeked. I wondered how many times Lee had put Jackson to bed like this. She leaned on me, let me, no longer angry. I was so relieved. It was a transformation, a miracle, like the way the pink dogwood held her leaves, held out, waiting for Iris to come and take her picture, the way Elaine came back in time to say goodbye.

# *Gloss*

We both knew it would be our last night together. In bed we first turned back to back, and I was comfortable with this decision. Then Iris begged me to let her touch me. So I did.

"I can't let this go," I said, afterwards.

"You have to," Iris said.

I wasn't crying, but I said it in a surprising broken way that must have sounded like crying. It touched off tears in Iris who cried a lot but never in front of people. I felt Iris's body begin to turn away. I pulled Iris's head forcefully to me, saw the tears and wiped one away. Iris flung her head around again, angrily away, so I couldn't see. But I could feel her body shaking. It was a quiet intimate moment.

"Maybe I'd feel better if I came," Iris said.

It startled me because she rarely wanted this.

"Maybe it would be better if you helped me."

I almost cried at that. I hadn't cared how it happened, but I didn't expect her to ask for this. Then I worried. What if I couldn't "help" her? What if Iris withheld, as she'd always called it?

I pushed the covers back and turned myself around in the bed and licked tears from the corners of her eyes. I went the distance it took to feel how sad I was. Just when I'd become familiar with the places and positions, now this knowledge would be useless.

"That's it," she said, at last. I knew what she meant. It was going to happen. It made me wonder if she was always in control, if she could've all those times she said she didn't want to. I didn't understand it yet, but I was beginning to get a grip on it, how it was different with women. Either that or Iris was finally after a three-day rainy drunk, sober enough to come. It made me really hopeful, for the moment. Maybe I could change, too.

But next morning it was not better. It was worse. I wanted to go back to Green River to say hello and goodbye to Elaine, Lee, Hannah, to everyone we'd found together, one more time before we went back to the city. Iris didn't want to. She wanted to go home alone, to go first. I was planning to drive back in the afternoon. She pulled the train schedule out of her pocket. She had it in her jeans. She looked it up. She could go at 11:11 or 1:00. It was a little cool but by 11 the sun was warm and delicious. We weren't speaking. I was roaming round, gathering and hunting, packing up. She was sitting with the schedule in her fingers, looking grim.

"What time is your train?"

"One o'clock."

"We've got time."

"No. Just take me to the station and leave me on the platform. I want to wait alone."

"No. Let's go to the beach. I want to see the ocean before I go home. We can be alone there. I'll walk alone."

So we went to the beach. Iris looked funny on the beach hunched over in her leather jacket, sitting near one of the slat snow fences, curled into her thoughts, angry or sad, hard to tell. Probably even she couldn't.

For an hour we sat separately, walked separately.

I could see that she could not be moved. Since she was going to have to leave anyway, she'd separated herself already. I didn't even know why I'd felt like seeing the beach one more time. At this moment the only thing I had was that there was no point and that didn't feel like a feeling. I went down close to the waves and circled back and made one more pass near to where Iris was sitting. She was still hunched over. She sat as far as she could from the pounding gray ocean she'd loved to photograph. Almost in the parking lot.

"Let's go."

"But your train isn't for another hour."

"Just take me to the station. I'd rather wait there."

"I'll wait with you."

"No."

We drove to the station in silence. I stopped the car but did not turn off the engine. I was mad now, finally. Turned off. She was so distant. I thought she was being mean. We turned to each other. Suddenly Iris pulled me close, hands on my face, kissed me deeply, broke away, opened the car and left.

I had no idea this was going to happen. Did she? I sat there stunned for a minute. She'd even put on lip gloss or some kind of sweet-tasting chapstick. The kiss remained sealed on my mouth. Planted. She must have planned the surprise. It took me back to that first kiss, with the Häagen-Dazs sticky sweet-ness, which had made me expect a dizzy new future. This one made me realize I'd taken only a taste. But something about her having put on something, even if it was only chapstick, made me expect she'd turn, wave. But she wasn't even in sight.

I backed out and pulled away and headed back to the yellow house to clean up. I stopped and got some paper towels and Windex. I treated myself to a bag of Charles Chips, something I would never get back in the city. I wanted to eat something salty. As I cleaned, all I could taste was Iris's kiss. How could I have been so dumb not to know it was coming? If I'd known, I might have been able to make her stay. At least kiss her goodbye, deeply, memorably; back. But she'd surprised me.

I got the first floor bath done when I surprised myself. I had to go back. I had to catch the train, kiss her back. I ran out of the house into the car. The clock on the dashboard said 12:56. Maybe it was fast. Maybe the train would be late. My pulse racing, my stomach churning, my lips burning, I sped down Three Mile Harbor Road, made the light at North Main, and screeched around the corner at Osborne Lane. What if I crashed? Perfect. Me and Pollock, together at last. Ding Ding Ding Ding. I heard the bells and saw something red flashing ahead. I made it across the first set of tracks in a burst of speed, but as I came round the bend the second set of gates came down as the end of the train made the bend and curved out of sight.

That's it, I thought, thinking how she'd said the same words last night, but they meant the opposite. The words now clamped around my heart and locked, keeping me from going forward, like the gates coming down as the train pulled away, without me on it, too far away to wave, to be seen waving. It wasn't the kiss. It was the gloss.

# LEE AND ELAINE

# Candy

I did leave him. It was awful, but I did it. It's now New Year's, two years later. Feels like two thousand. I got sick right after. The diagnosis was "a-typical GERD" (gastro-esophageal-reflux disorder) – you may have seen it advertised on TV. I still can't eat or drink hardly anything – had to give up alcohol, caffeine, chocolate, smoke, heat, drugs, dairy, wheat. I even had to eat starch and protein separately. Poe said the stomach is a tomb. On the bad days mine feels like a whole cemetery.

At least now I'm back again on the East End of Long Island for the winter, hungry for water. The *Tapestry* cover album just came out. We've already had one storm of the century. I've taken a different house, in Sag Harbor. I'm not sharing it with Bobby, or anybody, real or secret. It no longer feels like running away. Taking that part out of the equation is a big relief, though since I still have two places, I'm still on the road a lot. In my horrible expensive new apartment, in the car, at the beach, wherever I am, I am alone. I've taken a leave from teaching at Art University and am planning on writing this book for real.

I'm still not sure if it's going to be fiction or non, I spin ghost stories in my head in the car, but I'm also planning to interview real people to try to establish what kind of friendship Lee Krasner and Elaine de Kooning had. I'm still going to find out more about Green River Cemetery, find more women artists buried there and most important, find out if anyone knows why Elaine's stone disappeared, and then mysteriously came back that mid-spring two years ago. I have big plans. I have no plans, though, for New Year's Eve. Or New Year's Day.

But at the last minute, I get lucky: two great invitations set my course for the season, and, ultimately, the book. My friend Candie Boxx, who'd left the city too, found out I was going to be in Sag Harbor and invited me to her New Year's Eve party in Northwest Woods, another part of East Hampton like Springs.

"Low-key, just a few little rituals around New Year's," Candie said, "so bring something to make music with."

Candie is a video artist who animated dildos and she worked the art school circuit until the NEA cut that off, then moved out to Long Island to rethink her career options. I get nervous, hoping I won't have to take my clothes off. That's something Candie is famous for, not only on stage, but whenever. I think at least it'd make a funny story to tell New Year's Day at the older, more sedate, but with-it East Hampton art and academic crowd's late afternoon champagne and cake deal. My oldest best friend from high-school, Joy Gimbel, got me invited at the last minute. I feel anxious about going there too, feeling out of place twice, two different places.

It's snowing hard when I leave to go to Candie's. This time I leased a car, since I'm going to stay for six months. The roads are slippery. Again, I can't help thinking of Jackson's famous car crash, as I did that first winter I spent here, though I found out it didn't happen in winter at all, but August 11, 1956.

It's already forecast to be another bad winter, which makes me happy and nervous. I'm nervous as well about going to the party, being with people I hardly know, afraid I won't fit into this largely lesbo art scene crowd, but Candie Boxx is a surprisingly homey hostess. She'd spent the day making her special chicken soup, which is perfect for my restricted diet. The rest of the meal is great, though I'm not allowed to eat much of it. Too much garlic. There are lots of non-drinkers in the small crowd so I don't feel too weird about not being able to digest alcohol. I don't feel weird at all, until I try to talk about my book. Then I feel that familiar growing doubt gnawing at my already fragile intestines. No one seems to have even heard of Lee Krasner and Elaine de Kooning until I mention their husband's names, though the ghost story idea and the part about Lee and Elaine coming back as lesbians after all those years married to those macho art stars, gets, as usual, a big laugh.

By eleven thirty Candie has her top down, but everyone else is fully clothed. We do a sand mandala and have to make a drawing and a wish. Worse than taking my clothes off, I think. I'm in a panic and mortified at the silliness. When it's my turn I focus desperately on the colored sand part. I'm sweating. Moments pass. What do I want? I'm so lost. Will I ever find anyone again? Will I finish my book? Then I blurt out these words.

"I wish for something to happen that I can't even possibly imagine yet."

"Ooooh."

"In other words, surprise me."

"Aahh."

"Good one."

Applause. I'm pleased.

Slim goes next. Slim is Candie's new "wife," which confuses me. She seems like a sweetheart, but looks like a big biker. She wishes for "eternal love forever" with Candie, and to be a hit as Candie's new production assistant. Candie is leaving for Australia. She wishes for success and lots of money, not to be hassled by the censors and not to feel claustrophobic on the long flight to Sydney. Dinah wishes her new musical will find a theater and be a big hit and make lots of money. Suze is next. She also wishes for success and lots of money. Her girlfriend, Pam, a nurse, has had more wine than the rest of us and wishes, tearily, that she won't feel so self-conscious about getting old. I get teary too.

We have to do another round. I go blank again. When it comes to my turn I say, "I wish that everyone gets their wish." Everyone falls back, kind of amazed. They'd all wished for something for themselves. Money, success. Very New Age. They think I'm wonderful. I feel corny, a little too Old Age.

Then it's midnight. New Year. We sit around the mandala, the board that has all our combined colored sand drawings on it, and play a little tune.

"Let's take it outside and let the wind carry our wishes away," Candie says, "and then roll around in the snow and masturbate to orgasm." She giggles. I think she's kidding but I leave anyway.

Candie tells me to come back the next morning to start the New Year with a cleansing ritual.

Uh-oh, I think, now I'm going to have to take my clothes off. But it turns out she means we should all go to the spa at Gurneys Inn, in Montauk, the very tip of Long Island. Gurney's has a heated salt water pool with a view of the ocean, whirlpool, sauna, steam, terry robes, all for $20, the day rate. I can handle locker and steam room nudity fine. It's just at parties when it's cold . . .

I come back to the house around noon. They do a Tarot reading. I don't want my hand dealt, don't want to know. But what the hell. It's a party. A party game. But not for me. My cards: DISAPPOINTMENT, ANGER, DEATH. It's a New Age deck called "Voyager," and many of the bad cards have good names, but Death is the same.

"Let's go," says Candie.

I'm miserable about the cards I pulled. Maybe steam will help. At least I'll be all rosy for Sofia's party. At least we're on the road. Candie, Slim, and I are all driving to Gurney's in Slim's truck, scrunched into the front seat. Candie is trying to console me, to put a spin on the future I'd just drawn. But Slim is hard.

"Hey girl, I mean, fuck!" Slim explains. "No wonder you pulled those cards. You're writing about dead people."

"But honey," Candie says—

We're veering right onto Old Montauk Highway. That first sight of the whole Atlantic sweeps up and hits me in the face.

"—she's bringing them back to life."

"Yes," I say, trying to be positive, "I'm writing about heterosexual dead women who come back to life as lesbians."

"Oh my God!"

Candie's eyes open wider than ever. Her voice gets even breathier, low.

"What?"

"You're writing about you."

# Cake

After the swim in the glass-enclosed heated salt water pool facing the ocean, and the whirlpool and steam room, we go back to Candie's where I've left my car. On to my next holiday event, the champagne and cake late afternoon New Year's Day party at Sofia Willner's. I feel very festive.

I know the way, since I met Sofia, through Joy, the summer before. Joy has a place in East Hampton as does Sofia, though Joy rents and Sofia owns. Joy's little pool house is right on the railroad tracks while Sofia lives in a big house on Old Stone Highway, when she's not teaching at the Art Institute in Chicago or at her Tribeca loft in the city. Sofia knows everyone of a certain generation – all the artists – out here. She gave me lots of connections when I told her about my interest in Green River Cemetery and Elaine de Kooning and Lee Krasner. I loved the way phone numbers popped out of her head. I was taken with her. She's attractive, and intelligent, and with it, warm and willing to be helpful, like it's her project too. She's older than me, but much younger than Lee and Elaine's crowd; still she knew them. Joy told me she even went with Sofia to take Lee soup when Lee was dying – some kind of bad arthritis. And Sofia is social friends with all the older survivors, mostly women, some couples, the whole intellectual artists and writers scene. She likes the idea of helping me to get to all the others. Most of my leads, which I've yet to follow up, come from Sofia.

So I was thrilled when she told Joy to bring me along to her New Year's Day party, with her close friends, who all know all about Lee and Elaine. Many of them even knew them. Although I'm an outsider, feeling shy and anxious and, as a result, like I'm talking too much, it's so comforting to be where my Lee and Elaine and my Green River Cemetery are familiar subjects, even crucial to the crowd, as opposed to New Year's Eve at Candie Boxx's where I thought no one had ever heard of them and how awful that made me feel. I have a secret hope that, just maybe, Sofia might have heard of Candie Boxx, which would make Sofia perfect. But when I mention Candie's name at Sofia's party, there's dead silence. The story of the New Year's wish sand mandala, especially the part about going outside and letting the wind take it away and masturbating to orgasm, gets an uncomfortable laugh. Looking back, I realize that I didn't say a word about the made-up part of my book, about the ghosts of Elaine and Lee coming back as lesbians, to Sofia and her crowd.

The biggest coincidence is that Sofia also knew Hannah Wilke. It kills me that I only found this out after Hannah was dead. We would have made a nice threesome. I mean for lunch.

Sofia is in touch with Hannah's husband now. She always tells stories with relish, but her Hannah tales are especially juicy. Another woman painter at the party, a charming Southerner who has a loft in Soho as well as a place out here, tells me that her loft on Mercer Street backed onto Hannah's on Greene Street and when her boys were little they used to look across through the big windows and watch Hannah clean her loft in the nude. It thrilled them, she said, in her wonderful accent, but after a while they got used to it. She is a painter married to a painter too. When I tell her I'm writing about Green River she says that she and her husband just bought their plots there. I ask how much. The woman hesitates.

"$700," the husband says.

"Wow," I say. "What a bargain."

"Yes," he says, "but we're being cremated."

"Yes," the wife says, getting back into the conversation, "I always used to bring all my friends to that cemetery when they visited, to show them all the famous artists. It would be such a treat. But ever since we reserved our plots, I can't go anymore."

One of the other women at the party is a journalist, Louise Styne. Sofia'd told me about Louise the summer before, at our lunch at Grand Café in East Hampton. She gave me her number from memory. I even called Louise last fall. She had the softest voice with the broadest twang. We never did get together, but Sofia told me she was writing a ghost story too. About the same cemetery. Even some of the same ghosts. Louise had been involved in a big scandal with one of them. I wonder if they'll cross in our fictions. Spooky.

Spookier, the man she's with is a painter and sculptor who knew Jackson and Lee and Bill and Elaine well. And he'd been married to June Silver, who had written about seeing Lee and Elaine coming down Eighth Street together, the image that set me off on this whole chase. Driving home, I'm happy but also worried. I'm worried I'll never be able to write fiction, so meeting the real Lee and Elaine people is especially confusing. If I interview them, what about all the trouble I'll get into quoting them and what about all the crisscrossing gossip? I'll have to take sides, I'll have to lie, I'll have to leave out the best parts or go to hell. Worse: be banished from the Hamptons forever. I'll definitely have to change the names of all the live people in the book so they won't sue me or hate me. It'll be more of a ghost story since the people won't be real. Is all fiction really ghost writing?

# Co-op

I drove back from the party with a bunch of phone numbers
in my hand and the memory of promising to call these women
the next day. But when I got up the next morning, my head
felt like it was filled with mashed potatoes – I now know there's
a technical term for this state, "cottonhead," a peri-menopausal
symptom that is not really a bad thing, just some hormonal
activity that clouds your left brain for a while, letting you be
more intuitive. But not knowing this yet, I just felt paralyzed.
The stupid cards about my future – Disappointment, Anger,
Death – haunt me. And in spite of what Candie said, I keep
hearing Slim's remark that I got them because I'm writing
about dead people.

Instead I phone Stella Stone, hoping to leave a message
about how much I love her new book. Stella's a new friend,
post break-up, younger than me, a dyke, also a writer who lives
in the city. She must've been snowbound, too, because she
picked up. She asks about my book. It feels real in my mind.
She knows all about Lee and Elaine. I'm relieved that I don't

end up stumbling and stuttering about their husbands. But she seems to know so much more than me, which confuses the feeling. Still, it's gratifying to find a younger lesbian writer friend who knows the old, as yet not so in-again, straight AbEx painter world.

We talk about Lee and Elaine and how the Pollocks left the city to live out here. I blurt out how bad it made me feel yesterday when Slim criticized me for writing about dead people.

"What's wrong with that?" Stella says.

I feel better.

"These women need to be visible."

Much better.

"The Abstract Expressionists were the first generation of American apolitical Jews," Stella says.

"But Stella," I say, "they weren't Jewish. Pollock was a cowboy from Oklahoma. De Kooning a Dutchman. Well, Lee Krasner, of course."

"Helen Frankenthaler. Look at her."

I'm not sure what to look for.

"She was for taking away the NEA grants. And how many women participated in WPA projects?"

"I'll check. Maybe Lee."

"Wasn't Elaine de Kooning Jewish?"

"I don't know about Elaine."

"What's her maiden name?"

"Fried."

I feel proud. I knew this.

"Well, then, she's Jewish."

"Elaine Catherine Marie Fried?"

"Maybe."

"I'll check."

"Were the rents really that cheap?" Stella asks.

"Well, Lee and Jackson paid forty a month for their first house in Springs."

"I grew up on Tenth and University, before it was so gent-rified," she says.

"Really," I say, surprised. From her fiction, I had the impression she grew up in South Philadelphia. I think about the Cedar Bar moving to that block.

"Yes," she says. "There were a lot of artists there. It was all rentals. Then everything went co-op."

# The Cedar

My first interview is with Jeanne Wolfe, Elaine's exercise teacher when Elaine was already in her eighties – maybe after her stroke – if she had a stroke – where did I get that? I hoped, if Jeanne knew her well, she might know why her stone went missing two years ago, a fact that no one but me and Iris seemed to have noticed. Maybe she knew Lee, too. Maybe Lee and Elaine were in the same exercise class.

I called Jeanne, but George answered. She wasn't home. When I explained who I was and why I was calling he said he knew Elaine, too. He gave me the most fucked-up directions to their house. He said it was near Green River.

"Oh I can find it," I said. "I know a short cut from my house."

"No. My way is better."

Now I'm lost. It's snowing hard again. Very cold, slippery, dark. No street lights. This is not a street anymore. It's a road, supposedly Accabonac Highway, but I wonder if I've turned wrong and am now on Accabonac Path. I pull into a driveway where a light is on, skid and almost hit the fence. I get out and knock at the door. It seems like no one's coming but I can hear the TV. Then a large pretty young woman opens the door. I ask if this is Accabonac Highway. She says yes. I ask if Green River Cemetery is anywhere nearby. She looks blank and worried but not too scared of me. Not any more than I am of her. She opens the door wider. It's the country. People expect you to come knocking, asking for directions, even in the middle of a snowy night.

"Say what?"

"Green River Cemetery."

"Never heard of it."

"Thank you," I say, worried.

I get in the car, ready to turn completely back, head for home, forget the whole thing. But I drive on a little farther. After less than thirty terrible seconds, I pass Green River Cemetery, blanketed with snow. The woman lived right next door to it.

From there I have to look for a box number that George, the husband, warned would be hard to find. I pass it, then see it, skid to slow down. I don't see that there's someone behind me. The guy in the car swerves, curses, sees I'm a woman, gives me the finger. I feel I deserve that. Then he calls me a cunt. I know I should have signalled, but I hate when someone does that.

Jeanne is beautiful, delicate, bright red silky hair and fine white skin. Probably in her early sixties, she looks forty. She's a potter as well as a martial arts teacher. Elaine was studying with her, maybe that explains the green blob on the tombstone. But she tells me she runs a Tai Chi class, or some kind of bodywork workshop.

"Where'd you get such good legs?" Jeanne asks.

I'm wearing blue velvet leggings.

"I used to dance."

"You should take my class."

I want to. She brings me a drink. We sit on the angled couches, get cozy. A door bangs.

"Here's George," she says, jumping up.

A handsome older man comes in. I feel hostile at the interruption; I've already been cursing him for half an hour of blind, miserable, slippery pitch-black road. He's in a tweed jacket, like he's dressed for a meeting. I say so.

"Meeting you," he says, turning it on. I turn back to Jeanne. Behind her is a portrait of a young woman, her. George sees me looking at it.

"She was so beautiful when she was young," he says.

I hate it when people say that.

"She's beautiful now," I say. She is. She smiles.

I turn to beautiful Jeanne. "Tell me something about Elaine. How old was she when you met her?"

"I'll tell you an Elaine story," George interrupts. "I'll tell you what she was like. She was very aggressive."

Jeanne curls her legs under her on the couch. I reach for my drink.

"One day she's walking down Eighth Street and runs into Philip Lamar."

"Who?"

"A painter. A minor painter. Maybe she was writing about him. She wrote these 'impressions,'" he makes air quotes, "about painters, you know."

"I love that book," I say, though I'd still only skimmed the intro, pored over the pictures and the pin-up boys list, then I misplaced it entirely during the move. It's probably in my bin. But anger flares from me when he puts quotes around Elaine's written work, and the word "impressions." If she'd been a man he'd have called it criticism.

"I've read it," I lie.

"Anyway, they were in front of the Cedar. And Elaine is waving her arms and blocking his path, insisting they have a drink."

"The Cedar was on Eighth and University then?"

"Of course. So the painter finally breaks down and gives in," George goes on. "All right. But just one."

"Was it a career thing? A sex thing?"

I'd heard that in the book, *Elaine and Bill*, Elaine was said to have been very ambitious, that she had sex with important people, and, if George is right, not such important people, for the sake of advancing her husband's career.

"Probably a bit of both," George says. "So they go into the Cedar and they order drinks. Elaine orders a martini. He orders a shot of whiskey. Elaine sits on a bar stool. He stands. When the drinks come she raises her glass to toast and takes a sip. He's still standing, throws his back, and walks out. 'You said just one,' he says, walking out the door."

George pauses, smiling.

"She got what she deserved. She was so fuckin' aggressive."

He looks at me and laughs.

I want to kill him.

# Red House

But the bad taste George leaves in my mouth also leaves me hungry for more stories, more bits and pieces about the real women, though dead, who need, as Stella said, visibility.

But I'm not writing a book about painting. I'm not all that interested in their careers as painters. This is partly because I'm bad at talking about art, but more because I think it's hard to think about them as painters, the painters they might've been without the big shadows and light cast by their bigger husbands, who were actually two of the first real career artists. For me the burning question seems to be about friendship and competition between women artists.

Since I've left Jack and made new friends, or reconnected with old ones, almost all of them are women, a lot of them younger than me and many of them, for the first time in my life, are also writers. But not poets. By which I mean my new friends are writers who want to succeed. I feel competitive. I'm ashamed to feel that. I don't want to end up like Hannah Wilke, always complaining that I don't get the attention I deserve. So I want to know how it was for Lee and Elaine and their crowd, which had lots of women painters in it even though no one ever talks about them. They must've ended up in the same places – parties, openings, rooms, shows, husbands' shows. What was it like? Was it different then? Harder? It seems so hard now.

I get up my nerve and call Louise Styne, the woman who is also writing about Green River Cemetery and who lives with the man who'd been married to June Silver – the woman I wanted to talk to more than anyone. The woman who'd seen Lee and Elaine in the Village waltzing down Eighth Street in the sunlight during the late forties.

Louise's house is in Springs, near the cemetery, easy to find. It is still snowing furiously. The street lights and house lights and Christmas lights spark connections between flakes, between her and me, I feel, guiding me until I skid into her driveway, which is full of cars. I go in, and Louise and I sit. She already has some little nibbles out and some glasses and wine. We talk.

Maybe we're skirting the real issue or maybe we're really more interested in what we're doing now, live people, live women, not ghosts. She told me on the phone about a spec. piece she was doing on younger women/older men. It's an interesting subject. I always get hooked on younger people too. But they never seem younger. Jack was nine years my junior. Iris was younger than that, and a student to boot. But I don't feel it's my issue.

Still I want to get back to our original Green River writing connection but she seems to be avoiding it. Is she worried I'll steal her ideas?

I think it has to do with the cast of characters. East Hampton is still, for all its sprawl, a small town, especially the art crowd of a certain age. Her Green River ghost story involves one of the big players in the art scene – as big as de Kooning or Pollock, but a critic, not an artist.

I found his stone fairly early the first year I was exploring Green River. I remember it had some quote about art on it and then lots of Hebrew that I found disturbing because I still thought of these artists as worldly atheists, even if they were, as Stella suggested, apolitical. The critic was in a different part of the cemetery than the Pollocks or Elaine or Hannah. But discovering him was another big moment because, though unfashionable at the moment, he was a famous guy. I'd read him as a student.

Louise's book isn't a book at all; it's a play. It takes place in the cemetery. The characters in her story are all young women the critic's had affairs with, I gather, gathered around his grave. Maybe they're comparing notes, or hurling accusations at him. I notice I'm already imagining (i.e. writing) her book in my mind, the way some of my friends are already imagining mine. She doesn't give me any details. When I tell her I want to read it I find out something else our projects have in common, besides being ghost stories about Green River Cemetery: she hasn't written hers either.

Then her boyfriend Donald walks in. It doesn't take long for him to take over. She's clearly very proud of him, maybe part of the older man/younger woman syndrome. Maybe love. I've forgotten what that feels like, that look you get when the other walks into the room. I try to hide my disappointment. I'm having a good time with her.

Louise, getting up to serve him his Manhattan and cheese, tries to explain what my book is about.

"She's writing about Green River Cemetery and Lee Krasner and Elaine de Kooning."

"Did you know them?" I ask.

"Of course. I knew them all," he harumphs, sipping a drink. She passes him more Triskets and cheddar.

"Olives, sweetie?"

"Lee and Elaine, too?"

"Of course. I said I knew them all. Jackson would come over all the time to visit, Bill and Franz Kline and Ludwig Sanders."

"Do you know that name?" she asks me.

"No," I say, deciding to tell the truth. I like the way she's become my coach, my protector in a way, my guide.

"Yeah. He was a painter," Donald says. "He showed, was pretty well known, was a member of the Club, too. You heard about the Club?"

"Uh-huh," I can't help it. I lie. Well, I have heard about the Club, though I always thought it was a metaphor for this group of AbEx painters, mostly a boys' club, I imagined, talking intensely about art matters, in Bickfords or the Cedar Bar. I'd wondered though, if, even metaphorically, it included Lee and Elaine. I ask.

"She wants to know about the women," Louise prods.

"I'll tell you a story about Lee," he says. "She was very generous. One time she invited us out to stay with her. She's in a house near where the Pollock–Krasner place is, which is now her nephew's, and she gives June a beautiful nineteenth-century dress, doesn't fit her anymore. At this point she's a bit of a cow, but in the early fifties, before Jackson died, she was skinny. This was when Jackson was coming into the city once a week to see his analyst. And after he'd go down to the Cedar Bar and get drunk and start tearing everyone else apart, looking for fights and finding them, smashing glasses and getting thrown out. Lee was very thin then."

"The Jackson Pollock Ultra Fast diet," I say. No one laughs.

"Anyway, Lee gives this beautiful old dress to June and we go to the party. When we come home we see Bill in the road."

"De Kooning?" I say.

"Of course," he says.

"In the dark?"

"It's twilight. It's a cocktail party. Summer."

"Yes," I say. "Dusk."

"And we see Bill pushing this beautiful zoftig girl on a bicycle, and it's Ruthie!"

"Ruthie?" I ask.

Louise murmurs.

"You mean, Ruth Kligman?" It suddenly dawns on me. "The one in the car? I thought she was with Pollock? She was with de Kooning? Before Jackson or after?"

"After," Louise says.

"She was staying in the house next door on Fireplace Road."

"She was next door? And Lee didn't know?"

"She didn't know," he says. "And Lee is furious."

"Because she was Jackson's girlfriend?" I say, thinking I'm on track.

Donald says, "No. 'She's suing me,' Lee says."

"Because she owed her a painting?" I'm still thinking I have the jump on one of the other few things I know about them all, that Jackson promised Ruth Kligman a painting and never gave it to her and after he died, when his paintings started to get so much money, she sued Lee for it, but I'm wrong.

"For Jackson's accident," he says.

Dead silence. Really dead. I sip my watery drink. I've just started trying to drink again. It still makes me a little sick to my stomach so I only have a little at a time.

"Elaine was also very generous," Donald says, munching on another Triscuit.

"Especially to male artists," Louise adds.

"What?" I ask, trying to catch her drift.

"Especially to men," she says again, her voice strong. I wonder if this is supposed to be a snide reference to Elaine sleeping around a lot.

"Generous of her support, I mean, to other artists," he mumbles. He refuses to take the bait. I wonder if that meant Elaine slept with Donald, too.

"And to Lee?" I ask. "Was Elaine generous to Lee?"

"Oh no," he laughs again. "Not Lee. Lee didn't need her."

"Oh, of course," I say, "sure," but I'm not.

"One summer," he says, going on, "Bill and Elaine and Franz Kline and Ludwig Sanders rented this red house in Bridgehampton. You may have seen it, just as you come into town—"

"Yes."

I find him charming, actually, warm, soft-spoken like her, a good storyteller. I can see why she loves him.

"So this one time back at that red house in Bridgehampton, Bill and Franz and Ludwig invited Jackson over and he got so drunk he fell down and really hurt his leg. Lee was furious, said they were trying to hurt him on purpose."

"Jackson? You mean to take him out of the competition?"

"Lee thought these guys were trying to kill him."

"Jackson?"

"Lee was so damned paranoid, she thought there was a conspiracy."

He chuckles.

Now I want to kill him, too.

# Me(n)

I'm mad. Why are all these men making all my women sound crazy? Elaine was "so fucking aggressive," Lee was "so damned paranoid." I almost skid into a snowdrift on the way home, driving too fast. Maybe I should only talk to women. I keep imagining the same thing happening. I go to talk to some woman and some man comes into the room, dominating, driving the conversations.

Why am I so connected to these female ghosts anyway? I wasn't married to a big macho art star who oppressed me. I wasn't married to Jack at all. Had I been in some ways unconsciously inspired to keep my own aspirations low-key to match his modest achievements, a mutant strain of the same problem?

Was Candie Boxx right? By writing about heterosexual dead women who come back to life as lesbians, was I writing about me? I haven't had sex with anyone of any gender since the break-up. Do I qualify as a lesbian? It seems like sex is part of gender identity and having none makes me feel like I have none. Do I even want to be labelled? I never felt like any of the regular categories before. I don't feel like any of them now. I like that.

"Oh, you're so brave. To walk away from your happy home, your settled life, in the middle of your life," everyone said.

I am proud, but I'm scared. Will I ever find anyone again? Sometimes I don't recognize my body, like I have no body to seduce with. It makes me feel like a ghost, too. Maybe that's why I want to make Lee and Elaine – who were in their eighties during the eighties, when they died – come back as ghosts in my story, so they won't have to be self-conscious about their shape.

But I haven't been able to connect with anyone new, and really, can't write the first part of this book for the same reason. I don't know what to do with the part of me that had been with men.

The last piece of the old me, the part that couldn't talk, still feels frozen, firmly in place. That part that didn't even tell Jack I'd decided to go into therapy for the first time in my life, late that last spring when we were still together. I sneaked that, too.

I'd prided myself on being the only person I knew, except Jack, who'd never been in therapy. Our medical doctor thought we had the most no-stress life of any of his patients. All our levels were low. But soon after we made the supposedly temporary move to Brooklyn I started seeing a shrink. Maybe it was an excuse to go back into the city twice more a week, but I also was anxious all the time: I knew, without admitting it, that I had to make the break soon.

I shopped around. The first therapist lived in the Village, the same block where my parents lived when I went away to college. They'd lived in the Village when they were young and then left for the suburbs, first Jersey, then the Island when they had me. My father once lived in a building on Perry Street with Alfred Steiglitz. He saw Georgia in the hall. I tried to suggest to this shrink who had a haircut like Jackie O's, only bleached, what my problem was, as I saw it: I wanted two lives, a life with Jack in Brooklyn in the two-family house with his aging mother, and a life by myself in my own apartment in the city. And though I didn't say this or even think it too often, I wanted a place where I could have sex with a girl. I still ran variations of the Joel–Peter Witkin threesome idea in my head, but spread it out across two boroughs.

When I walked around the neighborhood in Brooklyn I felt like I was spending my junior year abroad. In Albania. It surprised me that they spoke English in the stores. Whenever I stepped off the train, or parked the car in Soho and hit the streets, I felt once again like I belonged. I wanted a place where I could be myself. But a different self. It didn't occur to me that *Three Faces of Eve* is about schizophrenia. I didn't realize any of this then. I just said the thing about two apartments and two lives.

"You can have whatever you want," the first shrink said, "in this day of design–a–life."

I tried the next name on my list. She was my age. I liked that. She didn't make it sound so easy. I liked that, too.

I started to see her twice a week, but I didn't tell Jack for months. I didn't tell the therapist I didn't tell him. I was afraid of the confrontation that might happen, but I couldn't keep making up excuses for these short trips into the city so I finally told him. It was as I feared. He got all panicky and said, "What's the matter, is it something between us?"

I closed down and said, "No, no no, it's nothing. Everything's fine. It's just me. It's just old stuff, my parents, how hard it is to talk about things."

"You sure it's not about us?" he asked.

I couldn't squeeze the truth out.

"Yes," I lied. I thought I was making it easier for both of us, for me, anyway. I guess I didn't want to talk about it because I didn't want to fix it, so to me, in my locked-down state, it seemed like there was nothing to talk about, which still left him in the dark, and me a liar. So, in my own darkness, hideous but familiar those months, that year, those two last years, really, I finally pushed things to the point where I made him throw me out.

And now that same part of me that couldn't tell Jack what was going on then – my therapy, my distress, my affair with Iris, my change of heart and sexual preference – now can't tell any girl I like about Jack. I still can't say to girls who make vicious remarks to me about hets that I was one, or even that I disagree. But it's starting to seem like the ones who talk hardest about men are the ones who always end up fucking straight girls. I don't have the nerve to point that out either. I still keep empty, quiet – feeling a stupid shame about my past. I feel like I am nobody, not even a writer, or only a writer who talks about writing about ghosts.

# Schindler's List

February. A dead month. The restaurants and stores are all shut, surprising me, scaring me, each time I find another one dark. I'm desperate to start writing, but I feel as blocked as my driveway. I walk into town and buy a light plastic snow shovel. I shovel my way out the driveway. The roads are always cleared by morning, and they aren't predicting snow for days. But it still seems dangerous to drive all the way into the city. Besides, something keeps pushing me away.

So instead of driving to New York, I head for the cemetery. My city. That feels safer, though I haven't been there yet since I came out this time and I've been feeling bad about that. But once I drive through the gates, I start to feel good, feel more. Elaine is, thankfully, still there. Hannah now has a real stone with lots of little stones on top, something I no longer have to wonder about.

The little stones are a Jewish tradition, something I learned from watching *Schindler's List*. Actually I only watched the second half of *Schindler's List*. I rented it from the local slacker's video store where they'd marked the boxes wrong. It was a long movie, two tapes, and I put the one marked part one in the VCR. I thought it was the beginning. After watching this tape, the second, not the first half, I was wrung out. I'd had enough. At the end, the people walk by and put little stones on the graves, a way of honoring, when you visit dead people you love. I guess it's a Jewish thing. This time I notice Ad Reinhardt has little stones too. I didn't know he was Jewish.

Lee and Jackson are there, as small and as big. Lee has little stones, too, and Jackson doesn't. That made sense. Then I trudge through the snow to Frank O'Hara. Ever since finding his grave, I think about Frank and the poem "The Day Lady Died" all the time. I feel so connected to him because of Green River and because I'd had the same experience he had seeing Billie Holiday's face on the *Post* when I saw Jimi Hendrix's face on it at the exact same newsstand in Murray Hill. But now I realize my affinity with Frank is more than that. Finding him made me realize he was my real connection to feeling like a writer. A New York writer. A New York School writer. Frank was the literary equivalent of the New York School painters, and when I started to write, and found my place at St Mark's Church, a bunch of second-generation New York School boys and girls, Frank was our model, our hero: his style, both in life and in words, cool and warm, breezy, toughminded and tenderhearted, like I wanted to be, even though I was never a poet.

As usual, I can't find his spot, especially with the snow. I walk around in circles. Finally I recognize the little bushes it was near, about twenty paces behind A. J. Liebling and Jean Stafford. I bend down. Because Frank's stone is flat I have to brush the snow off it. I'm not wearing gloves. There are the words again: "Grace to be born and live as variously as possible." Like fiction?

I think about how well Brad Gooch wrote about Frank's funeral here. It must have been something. I feel like I missed out on all the great funerals, Frank's, Jackson's, Lee's, Elaine's.

Hannah's. Now I'm kicking myself for not going to Hannah's, the only one I was actually invited to, but of course at the time of Hannah's death I didn't know I would become obsessed with Green River, in fact the very next day. My only chance left is Willem de Kooning. But it seems like he'll never die.

Maybe George will die in a car crash, on Springs-Fireplace Road, like Jackson, for saying Elaine was so fucking aggressive she got what she deserved, only unlike Jackson, there'll be no Ruth Kligman and friend, no women in his car. Then there'd be a funeral at Green River. In my imaginary event everyone would be there, even Whitney Houston. She'd be visiting Steve Ross. With her personal assistant, not Bobbie Brown. I'd persuade her to sing a special tribute to Hannah and Lee and Elaine, "I Will Always Love You," a cappella, standing by Hannah's grave. Hannah would put little bubblegum vaginas on all the stones, the Guerilla Ghosts would vandalize, desecrate, and rearrange Green River Cemetery, maybe putting Elaine and Lee side by side, making Lee bigger, making Elaine's stone more beautiful, making justice for women artists, and George, not Elaine, would, in my book, get what he deserved, for being so aggressive. And I'd get my Green River funeral.

# *Lee and Elaine*

Since driving's still so treacherous, I often take the Hampton Jitney, a huge omnibus, into the city, especially after I discovered the long-term parking system. I leave my car in the long-term lot behind the A&P in East Hampton, or sometimes in Bridgehampton, behind the Candy Kitchen. You can leave it for two weeks.

The Jitney's fun, like a big plane on wheels with a hostess, free snacks and newspapers, scenery flashing by. It makes great time. I don't have to drive the LIE. I can work, read, look out the window, though I miss the radio. I hadn't taken the Jitney in years, not since cell phones took off, the only annoying thing about it, besides the overcooling. But they've imposed a voluntary three-minute phone limit per passenger so mostly all you hear are quick pickup instructions, sometimes an advance order for take-out, or no starch in the shirts, a man calling to yell at the clerk at Brooks Bros. because his pants aren't right, sliming her, then asking to talk to her boss, then getting cut off. Big shot.

The man sitting next to me and I exchange glances. Until

now we'd avoided making contact, also like on planes, but this makes us both laugh. I get to telling him about my new obsession with Elaine and Lee.

"Lee Krasner lived in my building," he says.

My heart jumps for joy. Partly it's a recognition factor. This always happens to me when people ask about my book and I say the names to people. If they recognize Lee and Elaine without my having to say their husbands' names, something inside me soars. If they don't know who I'm talking about, I feel shattered. When I'm in East Hampton, Lee and Elaine are known, were visible, but once I hit the NYC line – on the LIE – they tend to disappear again.

"This was when Lee was how old?"

"Seventies."

"So she didn't just live in Springs?"

"No. One time in the elevator—"

"Where was this?"

"Seventy-ninth Street."

"We were talking, about Jackson of course—"

"East or West?"

"East. 231 East Seventy-ninth Street."

"I'm sorry. Go on."

"She was saying something about him I never forgot. That his work was this veiled image. He would paint it, then paint it out, almost out, and then build it up again and then throw this veil over it again and so on and so on. That stayed with me."

I nod because that explains everything, what it looks like, all that paint, drips, splashes. They're veils.

Next he says, "I always thought she was the better painter."

I try to remember what her paintings look like. No one had ever said that before.

"Me, too," I say. He deserves never to die. I want to kiss him. Things are looking up. Then he asks for my phone number.

Another time, there's another guy, an old friend from St Mark's, already on the Jitney bus when I board at 39th Street. There's that moment of recognition, then hesitation, then activity. Do I really want to sit down? Does he want me to? He already has a book open on his lap. I was planning to read the Lee Krasner *catalogue raisonné* I'd picked up on Spring Street. The text did not beckon. I hadn't looked at the reproductions, but I'd noticed a chronology in the back. That would be good. And convenient. But the old friend gathers his bags and papers up from the seat beside him so I can join him. Oddly enough, he's reading the Brad Gooch bio of Frank O'Hara, which opens with the funeral scene in Green River. So I tell him about my obsession with the cemetery and Lee and Elaine, knowing because of his age (almost mine) and his being another second-generation New York School poet, I won't have to explain.

"I met Elaine de Kooning once," he says. He has a lisp so it comes out oneth. "She showed me how to use chopthsticks."

This makes me feel better about sitting down with him. Maybe he'll be useful.

"I was in a restaurant, with Philip Guston and Edwin Denby. I was so young," he says. "She kept leaning into me and covering my hands, but the chopsticks fell out. She was drunk. Edwin and Philip kept looking at me, like warning me not to make fun of her. I was twenty," he smiles shyly.

I try to picture it, him, them all. They must all have been beautiful.

But then the nostalgic soft smile on his face shifts to a smirk.

"She was so drunk. She was such a fucking drunk."

Now I hate him, too.

# Artists and Writers

I learned that Bill and Elaine came out to the Hamptons later than Lee and Jackson did. They rented that red house in Bridgehampton, with Kline. Then Elaine and Bill separated. I wondered if Lee and Jackson would've split if he hadn't died, if she was already splitting that summer he did, when she went away, when she painted that black painting, and went to France. Maybe she knew he was leaving her for that girl, Ruth Kligman. Everyone says Ruth looked like Liz Taylor. Jackson had her stashed in Sag Harbor; Lee's friends didn't tell her till later. Her painting was called "Prophecy."

Bill was living right across from the cemetery with Joan Ward, in a house that had been his brother's. She got pregnant and they had Lisa. Elaine didn't like that. She went away. Then Willem built his studio on Woodbine, and Elaine had her own on Alewives Brook Road. Later Elaine came back to cure his drinking. She succeeded. Lee must've felt she couldn't do that for Jackson. There wasn't time. When Jackson was killed, Lee moved into his studio right away. It was so much bigger. Then later, she moved back to the city, and the studio and house on

Springs–Fireplace Road became the Pollock–Krasner House and Study Center.

Sometimes I wonder who I identify with. I get the feeling I'm more like Lee. That I could never be like Elaine – a beautiful floating social butterfly. A butterfly who drank. I love that they're both from Brooklyn. I've always had a thing for Brooklyn. Even during those windows when it's unpopular, I still wish I was born there. Not like some people, people who even lie about being from Brooklyn. My first husband came from Sheepshead Bay. He went to Midwood High School but said he was born in Dallas and was descended from Cardinal Newman. He pronounced it two words. New Man.

Elaine was born in Sheepshead Bay, too. She went to Erasmus. Real New York babes. Lee went to high-school in the city, Washington Irving, though she was born in Brooklyn, too. Her real name was Lena Krassner. But she'd taken out one "s" and changed Lena to Leonore by the time she graduated. She had different pretensions. Maybe because she was ten years older, born October 27, 1908, and so closer to the immigrant Jews who tried to assimilate. When Stella asked me if Elaine was Jewish I didn't think so. Why do people ask this question? Why do I even wonder? I don't care. Maybe I'm assimilating some of the anti-Semitism of the period. Then when I found out it was Elaine Marie Catherine Fried, I thought Catholic? German Protestant? She was born on March 12, 1918. Pisces, for sure.

Lee went to Cooper, but to something called the Women's Art School of Cooper Union. Then she went to the Art Students League, then the National Academy of Design, then Greenwich House. Solid credentials. She became Burgoyne Diller's assistant, head of the WPA murals project, which grabbed me, because when I was little my parents used to talk nostalgically about the days of FDR and the WPA. Lee started work on a WPA Abstract Mural Project for NYC. Then her part got cancelled. No funding. Even when the WPA was still getting money, they cut her part. Probably because they were women. Or Abstract.

Then, in 1942, Lee met Jackson. It was at a gallery show. Maybe they were both in it. They were married at Marble Collegiate Church, so she couldn't have been that Jewish. No one was Jewish in those days, especially Jews.

Elaine's background makes her seem less academically ambitious, a little more eccentric, eclectic, electric, more colorful, from an art point of view. But she did go to Hunter, then something called the Leonardo DaVinci Art School. She was going with Milton Resnick, a painter, fairly famous. I'd heard of him. But it was love at first sight with de Kooning, and they got married in 1943. In 1947 they went to teach at Black Mountain College together when Bucky Fuller, the Geodesic Dome guy was there.

My favorite Elaine bit is this: there's a big Hamptons event called the "Artists and Writers Softball Game." Now they write it up in the *East Hampton Star* as a big social thing, more than an athletic event. But I didn't know they had the Artists and Writers game back then. I don't know if it was called that yet. And this is the great part: everyone always wanted Elaine to be on their team. Why? Because she was such a heavy hitter.

Now you see why I'd have to identify with Lee.

# The Club

"Tell me about the Club," I said. "Was it a real place? Were there women in the Club?"

I'm visiting Louise and Donald again. I tried to see her alone, but she seemed reluctant. I got paranoid that she sensed my shift in sexual orientation and thought I was trying to hit on her. But she just didn't want to leave him alone. Maybe he, like my father, was not capable of fixing his own lunch.

"Here's the story of the Club, I'll tell you."

"At first," Louise says, "wasn't it at—"

"I'll tell the story."

"It started in," she says—

"A bar?" I say.

"No no no," he takes charge again, subtly, it's in his tone. We fall back, let him, give him his head.

"We'd all gather at the Waldorf Cafeteria and sit and drink coffee for hours and hours and talk about art and finally, we didn't have any money and the waitresses would kick us out so we decided we should have a place where we could meet, regularly—"

"Were Lee and Elaine in the Club?"

"Wait, I'll get to that."

"She wants to know if there were women in the Club."

"Let me tell the story," he says. "So we looked around and took up a collection and got a space in a studio on the second floor right across from the movie theater on Eighth Street."

"Weren't there two movies on Eighth Street?" I wonder. "The one near Sixth or University? I was in my first apartment," I say, embarrassed at going on, "across from St Mark's Church. I painted the steeple obsessively for a brief period. I became a painter because my husband said there can't be two writers in one marriage."

Silence. Then she speaks, sweetly, but with genuine interest.

"He thought it would be too competitive?"

"I guess."

"Your husband's a writer?" he asks. "Have I heard of him?"

"Oh no. I mean he's not my husband anymore. He was my first husband. He was a poet. I thought he was a bad poet. I felt sorry for him. So I stopped writing and became a bad painter."

I laugh. Then flash back.

At the time, probably inspired by all that expressionism around the corner, it looked easy. All you had to do was put on some jazz, stay up all night, pin brown paper to the wall, and use wide brushes and house paint. But I didn't want to say this to a real Abstract Expressionist like Donald.

It's quiet in the room. I feel stupid starting this whole conversation with Donald present. I could have it with her, about competition, about artist couples.

"You divorced?"

"Yes."

"How long were you married?"

"Three years to the day." At least, for a change, I'm comfortable talking about my history with men, with this straight couple, though I don't feel whole, or honest.

"You said first husband. You married again? What does your second husband do?"

"I divorced him, too," I say. "They were both a long time ago. I was married to him for three years, too."

"And then?"

"Then I lived with someone for twenty years, but we split up two years ago."

"Twenty years is a long time."

"Yes."

"And now?"

"Now I'm alone."

"How is that?"

"I'm getting a lot of work done."

Everybody laughs a little, relaxed. We sigh, sit back.

"So it was the movie down by University."

"Yes."

"I think that was the Art."

"Yes," he says, "and right across the street was a row of loft buildings that have been torn down, but Lee and Jackson had a loft there, and when my wife June and I moved from the country I tried to get a loft there, too. It was right after the war. They asked some ridiculous price and I turned them down, but later I found out that Lee and Jackson got that space for nothing. It was two doors down from Atelier 17, the famous print workshop, also on the second floor—"

"She wants to know if there were women in the Club," Louise says again.

"Now wait a minute. Let me get to it."

"Was Elaine in the Club?"

"Oh, sure."

"Was she—"

"No no," he shuts her up again. "I'll tell her the story. At first there were no women in the Club. There were men there who had, you know, feelings about women, men who said we don't want women in the Club. They were kind of down on the idea of getting women artists, but how can you put down

Elaine and Mercedes Matter, and of course Grace Hardigan came in as George Hardigan, but that's all the women there were. So guys were down on women. But Franz—"

"Franz Kline?"

"Of course. He says we're gonna have parties. Franz likes to dance. We gotta have women up here. Smart women. So for a while they would invite women up as guests."

"But Elaine was there always?"

"Elaine was always a member. She was always there. Everybody liked Elaine."

"And not just to dance? Any other women? Was Lee a member?"

"No. No. Lee had no use for it. Neither did Jackson."

"Not Jackson?" Louise says, surprised as I am.

"Well, he did not want to have anything to do with it." Donald does that chuckle of his, but almost a big belly laugh, at a joke I'm not getting.

"But why?"

He laughs again. "He didn't like the whole idea of the organization of it. He didn't need it."

It dawns on me that Pollock was already selling.

"When he was coming in from the country, he didn't want to go to the Club. He wanted to go to a bar."

"The Cedar?"

"Yeah, that was his bar. So when he came in the guys from the Club would go to the bar to run into him."

"Did the women drink a lot, too?"

"Yes," says Louise.

"Lee and Elaine?"

"Well, yeah, everybody drank. Well, Lee wasn't there. Elaine drank a lot, she was particularly high-spirited—"

"—You mean in the literal sense," Louise jokes.

"She didn't need the alcohol, but it helped her," he says. "We had great discussions at the Club, great panels."

"Well," says Louise, still trying to steer it to what I want, "what about Bennington? What about the Bennington girls. Didn't they come down—"

"Well, Helen Frankenthaler. There was a competing group about three doors down—"

"Really," she says, "I didn't know that."

"What was its name," he mutters. "Can't think of it."

"I'll look it up," I say, trying to cover his embarrassment at not remembering.

"What was the difference?" she asks.

"They were more intellectual. No parties. They had members like Barney Newman, Adolf Gottlieb. This was the uptown crowd, come down."

"Money," she says, "it's about money. Money. And class distinctions."

"But Bill and Jackson were in the same crowd?" I ask, to be sure I didn't have this wrong too. "Had Jackson already gotten recognition? Was he already famous?"

"Of course he was."

The way he said it, so sweet and proud, not competitive, makes me see how it was then, that if Jackson succeeded, it was good for all of them.

"He'd already exhibited uptown, Peggy Guggenheim was already buying him. Bill didn't show until some years later. He was forty-eight or fifty. First show he had uptown was with Charlie, uh—"

"Egan," she says.

"Ever hear of a painter named Pindar Pelitin?"

I can't believe it. He's talking about Grace's father.

"Yes, yes, as a matter of fact—"

I want to spill out this whole story, but stop myself.

"As a matter of fact," he says, "he was one of the first members of the Club; he was the bouncer at the door. If someone came with a guest too many times he'd throw them out. He didn't want women in the Club. Pelitin said we don't need women, and when we voted on who to let into the

Club he blackballed everyone; he didn't think they were good enough."

"Because he was European?" I say. I still can't believe we're talking about Pelitin. Images of him from when I was fourteen, his wild hair come back to me. They scare me still.

"Because he was a snob," Donald says.

It reassures me that Donald didn't approve of him either.

"Did he have girlfriends?" I ask. Now I'm probing. "Did you know his wife?"

"I met her once. Her involvement was—"

"Minimal?" I reach for a neutral word. I know Grace's mother abhorred the art scene. Probably because Pelitin did have girlfriends. Though she had one, too. Mrs McDaniels.

"She was very powerful," I say, hoping I'm implying something more.

"Yes, I'm sure she was formidable," he says. He must have heard she had a girlfriend.

"Did you know his daughter Grace?"

"Grace Pelitin? Of course I know her." He chuckles again. "I've known her since she was a little kid."

Grace at fourteen flashes into my mind. Was she ever little? Grace has a great laugh, too.

"How do you know her?" Louise asks me.

I don't know where to begin, or what version. I wasn't about to tell these people she was my first girlfriend. Maybe if it'd been just me and Louise, I could've told her, test the waters.

"We were friends," is all I say.

"Gracie. Funny you know her. Big girl. Deep voice."

"Yes."

"Now she's my landlord!" he says. He chuckles again.

# Life in the Big City

Grace, his landlord? As I drive home, my head still spins. What a flip. His studio, he explained, is in the building Grace owns, where she has her office, where she has my old letters in a drawer. I've been there a million times. My connections with him are already multiple: he's with another woman writing about Green River Cemetery; his former wife is June Silver who saw Lee and Elaine flying down Eighth Street as beautiful Amazons, the best of friends, which I can't get out of my head. But Grace? My Grace? His landlady? I guess she'd been my landlady, too. When I stayed on her farm in Vermont, first with Stefan, the Polish revolutionary and then twenty years later, three summers with Jack, though I didn't always pay rent.

It pains me to think of her. I haven't seen her in two years, since our falling out at the xerox store, right before Iris, when I told her I wanted to be with a woman again and she got all excited and thought I meant her. I couldn't call her. I felt humiliated for humiliating her. She even stopped saving my birthday horoscopes from the three New York papers. She didn't call me. I guess I felt relieved. Maybe, finally, it was over.

Yet, when I get back to the house, the moment I walk in the door, I find myself standing here by the window, with the phone in my hand, wanting to call her to tell her about this latest piece of serendipity with Donald Silver. Her machine picks up. I start to speak, choke up, then hang up. I don't want to start things up again, though I have such a strong urge to call the city. It would be nice to have someone or something waiting for me back there.

I have to go back. My lease in Sag Harbor is up at the end of April. I love this big house with all its windows, white curtains, sunlight and snow, stars, wind and, of course, the beach. I love living away, living alone, in a house filled with someone else's furniture where I can invent a life of my own. I don't want to go back to the city, back to my new, tiny, overpriced windowless apartment. It doesn't feel like home. I've hardly lived there, just a few months between the break-up and coming out here right after Christmas. I can't believe that now, in the middle of my life, my neighborhood is Bleecker and Macdougal where Grace and I hung out as teen bohos during the fifties. But Soho's just around the corner. Every time I go back, every corner I turn is a place I'd gone wrong, done wrong. I keep bumping into old mistakes, my ghosts.

I think about the last month in the yellow house, two years ago, the time of the pink dogwood, Iris coming out, Elaine going away and coming back, the kiss, the gloss. This year I'm prepared for the pink. I want to call Iris. I haven't spoken to her either, except one time, right before I came out here when I ran into her near school. I told her I'd left Jack. She looked astonished. She threw her head back and laughed, then said, "I can't believe you left him. I never thought you'd really do it." I can still feel how proud I felt at that big moment. She was the first person I'd told who looked jubilant, not crushed. At that moment I wondered if I did it partly to prove her wrong. At that moment I wondered why I didn't just fall into her arms and reconnect, start over, now that I was free. For one thing, she didn't open them. For another, I didn't want it. Still, I couldn't help testing the waters. I asked her if she had a girlfriend. I almost said "new" girlfriend but I was not sure if I counted.

"No," she said. "Now I only have sex with people I don't know."

Life in the big city. I don't want to go back.

# *Joy*

Next, I called my old high-school friend Joy Gimbel, a safe bet. What I didn't expect was that now, two years and four months after Jack and I split up, Joy, who helped move me out of Brooklyn, not to mention connecting me up with Sofia Willner and all those contacts in the first place, would come to my rescue again.

Joy and I bonded after her mother died when we were fourteen. After high-school we both went away to college in the Midwest, but we didn't see each other for decades. We got close again, come to think of it, when my mother died. Her coming back into my life – she bought an apartment right around the corner from my mother's – seemed like a great coincidence. Not luck, but fate. It would be perfect, since I spent so much time, then, at my mother's side, in Joy's new neighborhood, the Upper East Side. Joy was still renovating when my mother died, but not only did she come to the funeral, she helped me clear the apartment out, and saved my life again. That was almost ten years ago now. Since then we had dinner a few times a year. It was fun, easy.

I call her at work. We chat.

"I have no idea what this book you're writing is going to be like," Joy says, giggling, the way we used to giggle back in high-school. Once our giggling got us kicked out of orchestra.

"Neither do I," I say, laughing, now, too.

"I can't wait to read it," she says.

"Neither can I."

It's good to talk to her. We make a plan to get together when I come back. At least I have one thing pencilled in for May. And she'd mentioned she was looking for someone to sublet her East Hampton pool house when she went away, never expecting me to say I'd take it. She's there only on weekends so I could go out during the week anytime, plus she'll be away two weekends in a row during July which gives me nineteen consecutive days. Peak season, dirt cheap. So I have another retreat for a new season: summer. Her house opens Memorial Day – in my case, after the weekend – so I didn't have too long to wait.

I call Stella and tell her my good fortune. She always makes me feel good. I feed her my latest tidbit.

"Did you know Elaine de Kooning did JFK's portrait?" I say. "Drew it. Maybe painted it, too. She was a great draughts-person. She made amazing likenesses."

"How'd you know this?"

"I saw pictures in a book."

I found this out from the same book of Elaine's collected art criticism. I still haven't read it, except for the introduction with the image of Lee and Elaine together on Eighth Street. The intro said Elaine was the first artist – of any gender – to write about art for an art magazine, and the only one for more than a decade. She wrote about everybody and took Rudy Burckhardt along with her to photograph them. He took a lot of pictures of her, too. She looks so beautiful in them. It pleases me to see another person I actually know in her book. I'd bumped into Rudy at the Poetry Project in the city recently and told him so. He said he didn't have much to say about

Elaine except he remembered one such time when they went to interview Adolph Gottlieb and Adolph ended up chasing Elaine around and around the studio calling "Elaineschen, Elaineschen" as she stayed out of his reach. Rudy promised to give me one of his pictures of Elaine.

"There was a photo of her doing JFK," I say to Stella. "The JFK thing puts her into a whole other place."

"How'd that happen?"

"I have no idea."

"I suppose if you're in with the right circle."

"I suppose."

"Their worlds must have crossed."

Her words hang there. We both let them. Then she says, "You should call Betsy Westlake. I'll give you her number."

"Betsy Westlake? You know Betsy Westlake?" I say.

Betsy Westlake was friends with Lee and Elaine. I can't believe Stella knows her. Betsy, my latest obsession. I'd already fantasized about meeting her.

"I'll give you her number."

I'm envious. How does Stella know Betsy so well, feel so easy with her? She's younger than me but an old friend of all these East Hampton types. I've only seen a picture of Betsy, in a book, when she was young. She looks beautiful, like Elaine. She reminds me of Hannah, too. She writes, currently, know-ingly, for the *East Hampton Star*. Her by-line gives me a buzz. Everyone always mentions her, though they seem reluctant to give me her number.

Conveniently, Stella's planning to call her anyway. She says she'll tell Betsy to expect my call. It seems like such a coinci-dence that Stella should bring her name up, since I recently heard a great story about Betsy from another friend, Flynt Michigan, who also knows her. But then he knows everyone.

"One time Betsy and I are walking around Green River because she wants to check the ground cover on Frank O'Hara's grave," he said.

"That was her job?" I said, nevertheless amazed.

"I guess so."

"Her duty?"

"Her choice."

I wondered how that happened but didn't ask. I wanted to tell him about my connection with Frank, which was only in my mind but I didn't want to interrupt.

Flynt told me how they were standing by Frank's grave and Betsy said, "I'd like to be buried next to Frank." She paused and added, "but then so many people probably want to be buried next to Frank. It's so pushy."

He said she pronounced it in a funny way, like "pussy."

So here I am, my first day at Joy's, sitting by the phone, clutching the scrap of paper with Betsy's number on it. Even though Stella has just called her and told her I would call her, I'm terrified. I realize that I haven't even brought up Lee and Elaine's relationship with any of the people I've interviewed. Betsy would be the perfect person to ask. She answers on the second ring. I try to explain what my book is, but, as usual, I don't really know. I stumble.

"I'm writing about Green River Cemetery—"

"What?"

I can't believe she doesn't know what I'm talking about. I tell her about all the artists being buried there.

"Oh. Springs Cemetery. That's what everybody calls it. Nobody calls it Green River," she says.

"Right," I say, gulping, like I knew that. "And I'm writing about Lee Krasner and Elaine de Kooning."

"Oh?"

"I'd like to talk to you more about the two of them, uh, their relationship."

"They had no relationship," she snaps.

I panic.

"They couldn't. They were too competitive."

"Their husbands?"

"Of course."

"E De K and B De K. That's what they called themselves. Lee hated it that Elaine took Bill's name."

I'm thinking to myself that if Lee hated Elaine's taking Bill's name, they must've had a relationship, but I don't say that.

"It wasn't just their husbands, though. Really it was between them."

"Lee and Elaine?"

"Yes."

I'm tongue-tied, cursing myself for not having one of those Radio Shack mikes with the suction cup on one end, tape jack on the other, so I could record the conversation. I scribble skimpy notes with a dull pencil.

"I have a statement about Lee. That's what I show people when they ask me about her."

A statement. At first I'm shocked. It sounds political. Then, the real reason for my shock hits me. She, and probably all the other people I want to talk to, get pestered like this all the time. These questions, this probing, this intrusion. I don't know why it surprises me or why it took me so long to think of it. I'm not the first, not the only one.

I try to make my connection more intimate. I repeat the story Flynt told me about Frank O'Hara's ground cover.

"I don't do it anymore," she says. "It was impossible. There's no watering system. It's just grass now and I have nothing to do with it."

I feel put off.

"I'll send you my statement."

She doesn't want to see me. I feel the gates coming down. The warning lights flashing.

"You don't have to mail it. I'm out here, I mean I could come pick it up and maybe you'd have five minutes to spare."

"I'm very busy," she says.

I want to ask what she's doing that she's so busy. Maybe she's working on her column for the *Star*.

"I could leave it in my mailbox. After the mail comes. After two."

She gives me her address. It feels like a big deal. These names out here ring like the streets and boulevards in LA: Sunset, La Cienega, Melrose, Santa Monica. Here it's Springs-Fireplace Road, Three Mile Harbor, Further Lane, Spring Close Highway, Woodbine, Accobonac, Newtown Lane, even Main Street. I can hardly breathe. Like I've found something. Stolen it. It makes me excited. Why? I wonder if she's always lived there, how long she's been out here. Does she live here year round?

"Then, maybe after you've read my statement, we can talk. Maybe."

My heart floats up into my throat beating rapidly. Good anxiety. I'm going to meet her after all. Maybe. It'll be like meeting Lee herself, though in her photos Betsy reminds me more of Elaine.

"Yes."

"On the phone."

"Oh." My heart sinks.

"You really should talk to Esther Lazar. She was Elaine's best friend."

"Oh good. Yes. I will," I say, getting excited again.

"She knows all the gossip."

"Yes. Oh, good."

"And she's so much older than me."

Click.

# Betsy

Betsy's mailbox. Number 438. While my nerve is up, I call Sofia to get directions to Betsy's house. Maybe the directions are an excuse. I want to see Sofia, but still feel shy. I haven't seen her since March when she came from Chicago to spend spring break in East Hampton. Turns out she's busy, too. Still getting the house in shape for the summer and her kids' upcoming visit, but we make a lunch date. It's practically a year since we first met, after Joy introduced us last summer, and she gave me all those names and phone numbers.

Waiting until two, I follow Sofia's great directions to Betsy's modest house. I pull over across the road from the mailbox, with her magic number on it. I get out of the car, closing the door softly, not wanting to be seen. Or do I? I imagine she's watching, waiting, to see if I do come. Maybe she'll call out to me, invite me in. But she doesn't.

What if she's blown me off? I open the mailbox. Inside are two pages, folded over. I open them up, try to drink it in, without reading. It's about Lee. I skim. My eyes hold on to parts: "began asserting herself by spending his money . . .After the years of blue jeans, personal adornment suddenly hit her. She began to wear make-up. This made Jackson mad . . .the opening bars of the women's movement . . .a breathtakingly beautiful body, she got a sudden urge to buy a bra and girdle – absolutely unnecessary, but she desperately wanted to shed the ugly duckling image . . .a protester, picketer, petition-signer, fighter . . .after her assertiveness was liberated by the shrink. She had balls as a young artist in NYC, but marriage to J had squelched her. Remember, this is the early 1950s . . ."

This is going to be great. I want to leave a note but don't have a pencil. I pull off a bit of fragrant privet from a hedge, and put it in the box, hope it will speak for me, volumes.

# Stella

"Quite a courtship," Stella says, when I tell her about the pages, the phone call, the date with the mailbox, the privet, the note I left the next day.

"I'll have to put in a little Betsy Westlake trail."

"Yes," Stella says. "It'll be great."

"I want to get in that house. It looks like a little house behind this big hedge, but I bet it's not little."

"Well, it's attached to another house that Jim French lives in."

"I don't know who Jim French is."

"He was Frank O'Hara's lover," she says.

"Really?"

I notice there's this beat whenever anyone mentions death or love.

"But I really just want to get into the house."

"You do want to get in there," Stella says.

There's another one of those momentous pauses. I wonder about it.

"She has an incredible art collection."

Of course she does. She must. She knew everyone.

"Betsy was the only woman who ever fucked Frank O'Hara," says Stella.

The biggest silence yet. Something sinks, bringing everything else down with it, falling into place: Stella's earlier story about Betsy saying she wants to be buried next to Frank, her taking care of his ground cover. Even her suggesting how she doesn't do it anymore because there's no way to keep it wet.

# Esther

It was generous of Betsy, such a good friend of Lee's, to give me the connection to Elaine's best friend, Esther Lazar, even though she added that snotty remark about Esther knowing all the gossip, being so much older. Esther looked like some of the other women, women from the fifties almost fifty years later. Lee and Elaine aging has been captured in photos, so I'm used to the changes. She's still pretty and pretty old. Great lines.

"Were you friends with Elaine?" I ask.

"I was very close friends with Elaine. I knew her from the time she was eighteen until she died." Esther lit up with passion.

"How did you meet?"

"Well, we went to the same art school. It was on Fourteenth Street. It was called the American Artists School."

"Are you a painter as well?"

"Well, I stopped painting."

"You did paint?"

"A long time ago."

"Why did you give it up?"

"I guess I didn't have enough ambition."

I smile. She's smart and sweet.

"Elaine had enough ambition. She kept at it through thick and thin."

"I love her paintings, or many of them, what I've seen," I say, though I really haven't seen them, except some drawings in the book.

"Actually right now she's starting to get the recognition she never got."

"Yes," I say, though I didn't actually know this.

"But, she wasn't a great painter," Esther says.

I feel stupid for saying I liked her paintings a moment before. Why can't I be honest, like all these older women I talk to? What's the matter with me?

"No," I say, shamelessly inconsistent.

"But, she was consistent," Esther says. "She kept at it – and she was not like Lee in that she never sublimated her work, her affairs, to Bill, although people imagined she did. She never did. She did what she wanted to."

"Her artistic affairs, you mean?" I'm fishing. "Did she leave Bill for a long while and then come back?"

"She left for a long while," says Esther. I can hear the years pass, in her voice, too. "It's well known. They separated for many years. She came back only to help him when he was getting alcoholic. She came back then. Many people have given Joan Ward credit. There's no credit to Joan Ward. It was Elaine who did it. She came back and she stopped him from doing it. Maybe she made a big mistake. He might be dead now instead of a living zombie."

"Do you ever see him now?"

"No."

"Does anybody?"

"No. Just some caretaker and his daughter see him. He's completely out of it. He doesn't know anyone."

"Tell me about you and Elaine at eighteen."

"I came from the South and moved to New York. Then I went to the American Artists' School to study with . . .I know his name, but whenever I start to say it I forget. He's dead now. Anyway, he was the big shot at the American Artists' School. We all studied with him. And I met Elaine there, and she lived in Brooklyn. She needed a place in New York so she wouldn't have to go home at night. We shared several places together."

"You were all around eighteen? Wasn't Elaine involved with Milton Resnick then?"

"Well, Milton was one of the people we shared a loft with. The first one – not the second one. At the second one, Elaine was going with Bill. We shared the loft. She needed it because of her family, so she could stay over."

I think about how I got married to please my parents, to avoid confronting them about just living together.

"She came to this art school from high-school?"

"Yes. But she was a model."

"Artist's modelling?"

"Yes. She knew all the artists in New York already at that time. She knew everybody."

"That was just part of her nature?"

"Yes. She was a beauty. Lee was not a beauty."

"But Lee had a beautiful body."

"Yes, she had a good body. But Elaine was quite beautiful. She was really photogenic."

"Were you around a lot at social events and things where, let's say, Lee and Elaine were together? Did you all sort of socialize?" I ask, still hoping for the answer I've imagined to be true.

"Yeah, we did," she says. "But they didn't have much contact with each other."

My expectations fall.

"Do you think that was because of their husbands?"

"No," she says. "It just was that Elaine didn't like Lee and Lee didn't like Elaine – because they were both very strong women. They didn't jive at all. There was too much competition. It wasn't ill-humored really, but it was big competition."

"Because of their husbands?"

"No. Between them. They did nothing together ever."

"Even when they were older?"

"No."

My spirits are falling.

"Not even when they took yoga together?"

"It was Tai Chi. No. Elaine never had much regard for Lee."

"For her work, you mean? Or as a person?"

"Well, Elaine's also a painter, so there was competition. I never heard her speak about Lee's work. She never said a word about that. I wouldn't know what she thought of it."

"Do you like their work?"

"I think Lee was a very good painter, and I think Jackson benefitted tremendously from that. I think he was a taker, and I think she helped him a lot. I think she did sublimate her own work in order for that to happen – because she was born in a certain generation. Had she been born twenty years later, she wouldn't have stayed with him."

"Or maybe thirty years later," I say, trying to get myself off the hook.

"No," says Esther, emphatically. "Even twenty years. She didn't grow up in the Women's Liberation Movement."

It makes me cringe.

"Lee and Elaine were not similar really, at all. Except that they happened to both be married to the big artists of that period. I don't think that they would have had anything to do with each other if it hadn't been for that. There was a de Kooning crowd and there was a Jackson crowd. They didn't mix very well."

"And were you and your husband in a crowd?"

"Definitely de Kooning – always."

"You know Sofia Willner?"

"Yes, of course. Everybody knows Sofia. She's wonderful."

"Yes," I say. "She's wonderful. She told me about those two very separate groups – the way everyone lined up."

"Yes. There were real loyalties, not so much on Elaine's side, but if Lee thought that you were . . .she was very jealous of de Kooning and his clique or whatever you want to call it. She had her priorities."

"Elaine was less jealous?"

"Elaine had less to be jealous about. She really had nothing to be jealous about. She was very attractive, very well liked; she wrote art reviews. She was the darling of the art world for quite a long period. There was never a reason for her to be jealous of any of them."

"You were good friends throughout?"

"Yes. We were like sisters. I don't know why, but we just hit it off. We were opposite. I had no ambition whatsoever and Elaine was intensely ambitious. But she respected that. You know, she was an unusual person. I think Lee was unusual in her doggedness, and she was bright about doing what had to be done, but Elaine was by far the more interesting person. Lee was terrible really. She spoke to you in uncompromising terms. If you said something she didn't like, she would practically spit on you. It was difficult to be her friend. Elaine was brilliant and charming."

"Her writing is wonderful, I think. I loved that art criticism book."

"It's too bad. Her writings are better than her paintings."

"Yes, I think so, too. I think she really was a writer."

"But, it was easier for her to be a painter than a writer, because she couldn't sit still long enough to be a writer. When she painted, she always had lots of people around."

"Really? Right there?"

"She hardly did anything alone. She always had people around her. She liked that. That's why she wasn't a writer."

"You have to be isolated, sort of dead to the world . . ."

"Brrr," Esther shudders, half kidding, but it gives me an opening.

"Would it be hard to talk about her funeral?"

"I wasn't there. I knew it was going to be a big scene. There are some great funerals over there, you know. It's fantastic, that cemetery. Everybody got credit for my husband's remark. They all claim it. He said, 'They're dying to go to Green River Cemetery.' It's true. They bring their husbands' ashes and put them there. Stuart Davis never was out here. He never even liked the country. He has a large monument which they won't allow anymore. It's too tall. Then Ad Reinhardt's wife thought that he should be there with the great artists, but he hated it out here, too. Elaine's family put up a perfectly hideous stone that we all hate," she says.

The hairs actually rise on my arms, because we've gotten some place I'd forgotten I wanted to go to.

"When I was out here a few years ago and started this book, I visited the cemetery regularly," I say. "Then one day I came and the stone was gone. Do you know what happened?"

"Yes," Esther says. "They put this little thing that Elaine had made – this ceramic thing . . ."

"That greenish thing?"

"Yes. It was upside down. They had the date of her birth wrong too, so they took it down and had it fixed. We tried to get them to change the stone, but they wouldn't do it. We wanted them not to use that stone at all because I think that pinkish marble is so ugly, and with the green, it looks even worse."

"I always thought it was ugly." My voice had a little shake to it, though. It didn't help to feel I'd been right about that. "I don't think it looks any better right side up," I said.

"I think they just sent a guy out here and he moved it."

I couldn't believe it. She sounded so casual about it. I must have just missed him. What if I had seen him? It had given me such a shock then. This huge mysterious anxiety lasted years. Now it was happening again. You'd think getting the answer would be calming. I tried to change the subject.

"Were you at Lee's funeral?"

"Yes, I was."

"Can you tell me about that? Was that a scene?"

"No, not really. I don't remember anything spectacular about that."

"Her stone looks like a miniature of Jackson's."

"She was the first one in that cemetery to put a boulder instead of a stone. She got a man to help her get that big, big boulder – and they brought it there. The cemetery was a little surprised, but they couldn't say anything. And when she died, they just put her in front of it with a smaller stone. Now that they've opened up the back part, Jackson's hill doesn't look like a hill anymore. It reduced the size of his stone."

"I wish I'd seen it then," I said. I meant it. I felt it, but it wasn't a feeling of loss. A rush of contentment was filling me up. The direction the conversation had taken, by itself, was taking me there, like she was taking me there, back when there was no Steve Ross part, when Jackson's and Lee's stones were up against a curtain of black trees and vines, looking bigger. It took me back to all those pictures Iris had taken, to those first feelings I had about Lee and Elaine getting together, my original conceit.

"You know, I'm writing a ghost story about Elaine and Lee because the first time I went to the cemetery I had this fantasy that maybe Elaine and Lee came back as ghosts and were friends."

"Maybe so," Esther says, sweetly. "Maybe they're friends up there now."

# Sofia

"How's the book?" Sofia says. We're waiting to be seated at the new O'Malley's on Montauk Highway.

"I'm going to dedicate it to you," I say.

We're having lunch. Sofia smartly shuns trendy restaurants, but likes to try everything once. O'Malley's, while not new, had moved to a new location. It used to be in an alley in the East Hampton Village for years, a good bar, real drinkers' bar, and in winter, a fireplace. Now it's on the highway.

Sofia tells me that the old O'Malley's is closed, but opening again on Tuesday. Steve Ross's kids bought it. I found out his kids own Nick and Toni's – "the" eatery in town, not just for the Hollywood people, who are thought of by people as the new people even though they've always been here.

Sofia says Steve Ross's kids are turning O'Malley's into something called Rowdy Hall. It sounds preppy. I wonder why they want to call it that, but then I remember reading that Rowdy Hall was the name of a place where the local artists congregated, back in the nineteenth century. There was some problem about using the name, Rowdy Hall, getting permission.

I imagine if Steve Ross were still alive it wouldn't be a problem. Warner Bros. probably owned it, if not Time. I wonder if Nick and Toni are really the names of his kids. I wonder if, when they die, one of the one hundred and eleven plots Steve bought in Green River will say Nick and Toni's, like the restaurant, even though they're probably married to other people. More trendiness for my cemetery. I like the way Green River is keeping up with the times, staying alive.

"I was thinking of a title," I say to Sofia. "I was going to call my book *Green River*, but I ran into an editor at a book party. She asked what I was writing. I tried to explain. Lee Krasner, Elaine de Kooning, blah blah blah. She sounded very interested, which encouraged me because I'd just had another doubt episode a few days before when a younger writer I met seemed not to have any idea who I was talking about, causing me to lose hope again.

"Anyway, the editor asked the title and I said *Green River*. She said you can't call it that. There are twelve books called *Green River*."

"Really!" Sofia exclaims.

"I got really anxious, because I'm thinking how could so many people have stolen my idea, then, could my ideas be that stale, but maybe it's okay because I could consider one as a reference – all going through my head."

"Poor you," Sofia says, clucking sympathetically.

"Then she tells me they're all about this serial killer in Washington."

"Oh my."

"The state."

She laughs.

"So then I said maybe I'll call it *Lee and Elaine* and she said she thought that was a great title. So that's my new title," I say to Sofia, hoping she approves.

Sofia gets a serious look. "You could call it *The Artists' Cemetery*. That's what everybody calls it."

"They do?" I say, brightly, trying to hide my confusion since when Betsy Westlake said she'd never heard anyone call it Green River, she said that everybody called it Springs Cemetery. But Sofia is my teacher, so the correction feels good. "That's a great title. I will. I'll call it *Artists' Cemetery. Artists' Cemetery* is a great title."

"Did you ever get in touch with June Silver?" Sofia asks. "June doesn't like me, you know."

"I do know. Because you're friends with Louise."

She told me this the first time I asked her for June Silver's phone number. It was the first time Sofia hadn't come through. I was sure she had or could get June's number, but she clearly didn't want, this time, to be the connector. It was a matter of social etiquette. June had been married to Donald Silver, of Louise and Donald. She still had his name. Still, I thought there was more to the rift between June and Louise than sharing a mate. I'd found out more about Louise. Her affair with the critic, the guy with the Hebrew graffiti on his tombstone, had stirred up an awful lot of trouble. But she and Donald seemed happy now, domestic. Hard to imagine the whole community up in arms, taking sides.

"Those things don't die," says Sofia. "June hates Louise almost as much as May."

I don't know who May is. Maybe the big critic's wife. I wonder if Sofia could tell by the blank expression on my face.

Luckily the waiter comes by to take our drink order and tell us the specials.

"Well, Jason Hook will know June's number. He can connect you," she says. "Did you call him?"

"Yes," I say.

I'm seeing Jason Hook next week. Sofia set it up, as usual. She even called him for me. But I still feel a thrill rise, knowing I can say yes and it'll be the truth. This time, in my new house, in this new green summer season, I'm following through. Not so scared.

The waiter returns with the drinks.

"You have a nice club sandwich," Sofia says, thinking she's ordering.

"Yes. But not today."

I remember our first lunch now at the Grand Café on Newtown Lane in East Hampton last summer. She had the club sandwich. Did I already have my bad stomach then? It didn't start until after Jack and I broke up. These last few years have been so confusing.

"I'll have the grilled chicken Caesar salad," she says.

"Is there garlic in the Caesar?" I ask.

"On the croutons."

"Could I have no croutons? And my dressing on the side?"

"People took sides," Sofia says.

"You mean—"

"Yes—"

"Between Harold Rosenberg and Clement Greenberg?"

I know little about these two giants. I think Clement Greenberg was pro-Pollock, his champion, and Harold Rosenberg was de Kooning's guy, the first to write about and recognize him. Greenberg was the one who coined "Action painting," but he's not buried out here.

"They did," says Sofia. "Yes. Between Pollock and de Kooning and other people lined up behind them. You know that whole crowd, the people, they just idolized him."

"Jackson?"

"Yes."

"His painting?"

"As a man. You know, the ultimate artist–hero. And all those guys around Pollock – and de Kooning for that matter – were drinkers."

"The women, too?"

"Not so much. But I think that's why they all got Alzheimers. That and the oil paint, turpentine, all the fumes. But mostly the alcohol. They all had it, de Kooning, of course, James Brooks before he died. And Philip Rivers. You should talk to

Caroline Rivers. She and Phil were friends with Lee and Jackson," she says, and rattles off the number from memory.

"I already talked to her," I say, proud again, "after you told me to call her the first time. I went to her house. It's so beautiful. I love how she stained the floors green."

"She's a wonderful artist, too," Sofia says.

"Yes," I say. "She showed me her work. It was in the bedroom."

"Typical."

"But here's the thing. It turned out that she was my teacher when I was thirteen and going into the Museum of Modern Art on Saturdays for art classes."

"That's wonderful," Sofia says, genuinely amazed. "Small world."

I still couldn't quite believe it either. Until recently I hadn't thought about that time, being in high-school in the suburbs, then meeting Grace and falling in love with a girl who grew up in the Village and falling in love with the city and with all the new painting and going to the Modern and even remembering this pretty woman who brought in hot pink net and sequins for us to make collages with and how long I kept the one I made and now I've just met her again almost half a century later.

"She said Lee and Elaine were friends in the early days."

"It's possible. Who else."

"Caroline told me to talk to Flora Upton. She said she told Flora I was coming over to talk about Lee, and Flora said, 'Well she should talk to me. I know much more about Lee than you do.' "

"That sounds like Flora. Flora was a much more interesting painter than her husband," Sofia says.

"Caroline told me that Flora and Lee and Betsy Westlake used to go into the city once a week for therapy, and they called it something funny, but she couldn't remember what but Flora said they called the train 'the flying couch.' "

"Oh, yes," Sofia says. "That's a famous story."

"Did you hear the one about Lee and the egg in aspic?"

"You mean when someone questioned whether Jackson should show in Germany because they thought he was Jewish and the egg slipped out of Lee's hand onto her beautiful suit? Of course."

Sofia knew everything. She was the first person to question my theory that Hannah and Eva Hesse and other women artists who worked with latex died because of it. I like theories about death.

She'd said, "I think, in Hannah's case, it was the killer ceramic dust."

Sofia and I got along right away. We have certain things in common, aside from our interest in these women, this scene. We both teach liberal arts in an art school. She has a loft in Tribeca, which she now sublets. I had a loft in Soho, which Jack and I sublet while we were in Brooklyn. She is now thinking of giving up her loft, selling it. I gave up our loft. I, like a fool, let our loft go. What insanity. It was prime Soho real estate, 2000 square feet on Greene between Spring and Broome for $700 a month. Since Jack and I split everything, my rent for this primo location was $350. Jack and I'd lived there so long we probably had the last unreconstructed loft in Soho. I'd relished the bargain, the low overhead, the high ceilings. Fourteen feet. The original tin. And when Jack and I finally did break up no one asked what happened to us. No one said how come such a perfect couple split up? After twenty-two years? The first thing everyone asked, like it was the real tragedy was – what happened to the loft?

"How are you ladies doing? Would you like some more ice tea?"

"It's free," I say to Sofia. I'd gotten there so early I'd memorized the menu.

"Well," says Sofia, "if it's free. Could you bring a pitcher?"

I picture years of her entertaining all these friends, in her garden, pitchers of ice tea, picture artists drinking the tea, women.

"I'm sorry. We only do pitchers of beer."

"Well, then, could you bring me a fresh one, in a fresh glass?"

"Sure can. How 'bout you?"

"Can I have another glass of water? I mean more water. In the same glass is fine, though."

We eat for a while while I update her about Betsy Westlake.

"You know Frank O'Hara has a Betsy Westlake poem," she says.

I can't believe she mentions Frank O'Hara. I didn't know he had a Betsy Westlake poem. But I don't say that. Instead, for a change, I listen. I don't interrupt.

"It's a nice poem," Sofia says. "You should know it."

"Oh, yes, I should. I'll look for it."

"Yes. It's about him going out to East Hampton to visit Betsy Westlake. He's walking around the city on his way to the station. He picks up some wine, some flowers. That's where he's going. He's going to visit Betsy Westlake," she says.

My neck hairs rise. Frank writes a poem about visiting Betsy Westlake. I visited Betsy Westlake. At least her mailbox. I feel like I'm swimming but not drowning. Frank O'Hara and Betsy. He writes a poem about her. She wants to be buried next to him in Green River. Everything's coming together, like the book is writing itself, without a writer, a dream book. I want to leave it hanging, all connected, for a delicious moment. I know I can't do that. There's more.

"Yes," Sofia said. "It's a lovely poem. It's called 'The Day Lady Died.' "

# Lost

You know how in Medieval and Renaissance manuscripts "f"s and "s"s look reversed? I remember a line in a sonnet by a minor poet, Samuel Daniel, when I was in grad school which looked, on the page, like "All are men and all have fucked their mothers" when it really was about breastfeeding. Well, whenever I think of the word "loft" now, it seems like "lost." The story of how I lost the loft still haunts me.

Since that day I started school and Iris was in class, since that week that Jack was in the hospital and I was so happy to be alone, since the time, the next fall, I persuaded him that we should leave Soho and go live in Brooklyn with his mother, I knew I needed to leave Jack.

A bizarre plan. Art couple leave their Soho loft and move into a two-family brick with the guy's Old World mother? Why would they do that? Why in the world? There was only one person who knew the answer and she wasn't talking. Until now.

Part of me wanted to leave the scene, to move, change places. I even liked the feel of the small Brooklyn houses near the stinking industrial flats of Newtown Creek. Over the years, when we'd take the bus out, I'd project living there – after all these years of the Village, East, West, Soho – and feel it'd feel good to feel strange. That was the part I could talk about even though no one believed I could ever live anywhere other than Manhattan.

I imagined that if I moved us both out to Brooklyn, to this exile on Flatbush Avenue, I could get him settled above his mother and slip out the back door. He wouldn't notice I was leaving him; he would be happy to be living in Brooklyn, a million miles from his friends, his work, his life, with his mother. I thought this plan would work. For me, anyway. At the moment, it was the only one I could handle, easier than speaking, than sitting down, getting drunk, whatever it took to have the conversation about needing to leave, to be on my own, to end the relationship, to change it, to have a girlfriend, to have a scene with Jack, rage, tears, silence, misery. But have the conversation. Have it in Manhattan. Preferably Downtown.

Crazy? Well, maybe, but also, in a way, a simple plan. Because by the end of the summer, Jack's mom was afraid to be alone. She got confused, nervous, she called it. Moms worried. Jack worried. I worried, but I still wasn't ready to talk about the real problem so I tried to solve the immediate one. I said, "Hey, why don't we move in with your mother. We could sublet the loft to some of my students who'd die to live in Soho even for a year. Then you won't have to worry about her."

"You'd do that?" he said. He was thrilled I was being so nice.

"We'll take her to a doctor and have her tested and see what's really going on, and if she needs more care or treatment or something we'll deal."

And so we did. That is, he did. I had agreed to teach four classes so I convinced him I had to stay on in the loft alone, but only for a few months, and then I'd move into Brooklyn with Jack and the students would sublet the loft.

That was my plan. Jack moved to Brooklyn. He begged me

to come. I used my excuses. He had no furniture, just an old mattress and a lamp on the floor. Every night on the phone he cried about his mother, but he wouldn't come into the city to visit me. I pretended to pout. He said he was afraid to leave his mother alone, because she got confused. I was confused, didn't think yet, maybe he was as confused, as scared to confront what felt like some impending parting as I was. His resentment about my full-time teaching grew.

"Your students are ruining our life," he said, in tears, during one of our nightly phone calls.

I called twice a day, every day. I was busy, happy, alone.

Well, not exactly alone.

I'd accepted a dinner invitation from Agnes Morgan. At least she wasn't my student. Jack and I had met Agnes and her glamorous girlfriend Arlene at a party during the summer, a month after Iris and I had our final fight. I was just getting back on an even keel. Still, something happened the moment I laid eyes on Agnes. She was tall and flat and wiry. She had a great haircut. And her manner, tough and seemingly vulnerable simultaneously, got to me. She got to me like Iris had. But she was not an artist. Agnes was an ambitious broker who was just starting her own business. She was conservative and conventional. She was a jock. She liked the North Fork, not the South. She hated the Hamptons. She had a girlfriend. They talked about the house they were buying, which seemed kind of perfect. Maybe she'd want to sneak around, too.

Over the summer all we did was exchange a few letters and books. She asked me to send her my books. She sent me some of her favorites, books with feminist if not lesbian themes. She had a thing for writers. It flattered me that she was interested. She liked writing letters, which was unusual and charming. I liked writing back. Jack and I spent August in Noyac. She was on Orient Point, across Peconic Bay. One day I took the car and the ferry across and tried to find her house. I think I did find it. I drove around the cottage, caught a glimpse of her head in a window, waited for an hour, got cold feet and went back to Jack. Then, after Jack moved out to Brooklyn and I was by myself in the loft, she started calling twice a day from her office.

By late October, we'd picnicked at the Cloisters, kissed on Bedford Street, sipped a hundred dry martinis, done everything but fucked because Agnes, a professional in every sense, had to break up with Arlene, her girlfriend of many years, first. They'd just put a payment down on a house. So she had to get her money back, too. So we waited. Waiting was sexy. It made me feel, in a sick way, innocent. I ain't done nothin'. Yet.

Finally, school was almost over. I couldn't put Jack off forever, so I started to pack. I knew I wanted this woman. Another woman. It was clear that this, if not this particular girl, was it. Agnes, finally technically separated from her girl-friend, was ready, technically, for me. The day after the break-up, a few days before Thanksgiving, we fucked furiously until the phone rang. She answered it. I couldn't believe it. It was the girlfriend again, not ready to quit. I was filled with post-sex euphoria and endorphin spill and generously volunteered to leave. Besides, I had to pack.

As I put things in boxes, some marked "Brooklyn," some marked "stay," I knew I shouldn't move out of the loft. I knew I had to talk to Jack and tell him it was over, but I couldn't. I moved to Brooklyn. With furniture. But I couldn't stay put. Twice the first week I ran back to the city, trying to figure out excuses to stay over with Agnes.

"Why do you have to stay over? It's a $10 cab ride," he said. I had no answer. I went to the city and came home again.

Jack and I bought a car. I drove into the city. Parking was expensive. Agnes and I went to a movie. I'd told her I was staying over. But I hadn't told Jack. We bumped into an old friend of mine and Jack's in the lobby and I panicked, afraid he'd tell Jack I was with Agnes. I couldn't concentrate, so we left halfway through the movie and went to her place. After we had sex, Agnes seemed surprisingly relieved that I'd changed my mind and was leaving to go back to Brooklyn.

The next time I realized Agnes was just as jumpy as I was, always looking over her shoulder, going to way, way out of the way places.

"Didn't you tell her it's over? Isn't it over?" I asked.

"I did. I took all my sweaters back. It's over. It's nothing."

"What are you afraid of?"

"I'm afraid she'll see us."

"Why?"

"I don't want to hurt her."

"When did you get your sweaters? Did you see her?" I knew they had each other's keys. "Was she there?"

"Yes."

"What happened?"

"She cried."

"Did you have sex?"

"Well," Agnes said, her eyes filling with tears, "she was so unhappy. She had sex, if you know what I mean."

I knew what she meant, but I was still jealous. "I thought you broke it off."

"I did. I'm just afraid she'll do something."

"What do you mean 'do something'?"

I was getting madder by the minute.

Agnes was crying now.

"Like kill herself?" I asked.

I went home again. The closer I got to Brooklyn the better I felt. I vowed to break this off. I even pulled over onto an exit ramp of the BQE to write it in my journal, signed and dated. It wasn't worth it. It felt like it would never work with Agnes anyway. I kept imagining that if I found the right woman, she would sweep me off my feet, we would fall madly in love, I would have no choice but to leave Jack, no choice but to tell Jack. That's what happened with my second husband. When I met the Polish revolutionary. Though even then I had to be on LSD to tell the truth.

But I didn't really want that this time. I didn't want another entanglement. I wanted to be alone. I didn't want to leave Jack for someone else. I loved him too much to hurt him that way. It was bad enough cheating on him. That's why I felt so good heading home, away from her. I was unhappy enough already, knowing I had to turn my whole life upside down and being afraid I would never have the guts to do it. I couldn't stand the added tension of seeing Agnes. The way the cheating and sneaking and lying, especially to myself, lurked under the surface of my new desires.

The next day the phone rang. It was Agnes, calling from her office, whispering so her assistant wouldn't hear. She sounded frantic. I was whispering too, behind the thin door of my room.

"What's happening?"

"It's Arlene."

"So?" I said, annoyed.

"Something's going on. I just got the scariest call."

Agnes said a man had called. A voice she didn't recognize.

"He said, 'You stay away from my wife or I'll kill you. Arlene told me everything.' "

Agnes started to cry.

"What did you say?"

"Nothing. He hung up." She was sobbing, then the phone was quiet. I knew she was crying more.

I felt bad for her. It didn't feel like it had anything to do with me. Yet.

"You didn't recognize the voice at all?"

"It must've been Jack."

I laughed out loud. Involuntarily. I was certain it couldn't be Jack. In the first place, he didn't know. He didn't even know Arlene's name. He'd only met her once, at that party. We'd met as couples. Besides, Jack would never do anything like that. He didn't threaten. He was direct, not a schemer. He wasn't the type. And, most important, he would never call me his wife. We'd always been clear on that. The only time I'd ever called him my husband was when they rushed him to the VA hospital.

"It couldn't be Jack. He would never do that. Nothing's

going to happen. It's probably some crank call. Maybe Arlene got some friend to call, just to harass you. Just because she's feeling rejected and angry." At that point it was starting to make me very nervous too. But I said, "Don't worry."

"I can't help it," she hiccoughed, like a little girl. She blew her nose. I could picture the handkerchief she always carried.

"Maybe it was a wrong number," I said.

But when I got off the phone I started to pace. Agnes wouldn't want to have anything to do with me now. Would that be good or bad? For the next two days I worked up a phony story so I could stay over in the city. I told Jack I had plans to go to the theater but had to take my manuscript to a literary agent early in the morning the next day. I pretended it was tickets some student had given me to something Jack would never want to see.

"You remember Iris, my student?"

"Whatever happened to her? She never calls you anymore."

"Oh, I know and thank God! That's the thing about students, baby. Once class is over, they disappear.

"Anyway, I bumped into her and she's going away this weekend and she said I could crash at her pad, her flat she calls it. I have to be at the agent's so early Monday morning. I have the keys."

I jingled the keys. I was starting to loathe myself, but running on autopilot, racing down the familiar fast lane of the LIE. The scene with the realtor, me tied to that four-poster bed. The gesture I hadn't seen, or hadn't heard in so long.

"Just this once. I promise," I said, and kissed him goodbye. He let me go. No fuss.

"I'm going to the play with Agnes," I said. "You remember Agnes. The stockbroker?"

"She was nice," Jack said. "Her and her girlfriend, we should have dinner with them sometime."

"Yes."

Of course there was no play. Agnes and I were having dinner. Afterwards we cabbed to her place on the Upper West Side.

It was the first time we'd spent the night together since I'd moved to Brooklyn. I felt like a criminal, which was sexy. We drank. We took a quick scented bath. I came to bed in a robe. When Agnes slammed me down on the bed I slipped the sleeves off my shoulders and the rest undid itself. The robe lay on the bed, damp and crumpled underneath me while we had sex. I was in the middle of coming when Agnes said,

"What's that?"

"What's what?" I giggled.

"What's that?" Agnes said again, turning her head.

What's wrong with you, I thought. "It's me," I whispered. I laughed, expecting some transforming moment of contact because I'd said words. But Agnes didn't hear me. I was baffled. She got up and went to the bedroom door. Then she opened it quickly and slammed it behind her. I was in a daze, flushed, fulfilled, not even listening fully for a few seconds.

Then I heard voices.

"You can't come in here." (That was Agnes.)

More noises, the voices getting closer, and sounds, like someone pushing and shoving Agnes. The bedroom door was closed, but I could tell someone was in the apartment. The sound Agnes had heard must have been the key in the front door lock.

I wanted to shout out, ask Agnes if she was okay, but I was paralyzed, caught in a nasty flood of endorphins and anxiety. Could some guys have broken into the apartment, to rob it? Were they hurting Agnes? I got up, looked for something to use on them. Then I heard the other voice. A girl's voice.

"Arlene," Agnes said. "Arlene," she said again, plaintive, frantic, possibly angry. "You can't do this. You have to leave."

Arlene. It was Arlene. Lovely hurt Arlene. The scuffling was getting closer, more frantic. I heard a lamp fall and break. Then both of them banging against the bedroom door.

"Arlene. You can't go in there."

"The wife! The wife! It's the wife!" Arlene screamed.

I thought of yesterday's phone call, Agnes's panic about it.

"You leave my wife alone or I'll kill you." Could Arlene have made it? Disguising her voice electronically? She knew Laurie Anderson. Or was Agnes also involved with someone else's real wife? At this moment anything seemed possible. Something crashed to the floor and scattered. I felt like Agnes was protecting me, trying to keep my identity private, trying to keep Arlene out of the bedroom, like an animal defending the lair of her cubs. It made me feel loved. But maybe she was protecting her reputation.

I wondered about that. Agnes was strong. She went to the gym all the time. She was always giving me her muscles to feel. Agnes could have immobilized Arlene, despite hysterical adrenaline fury. After a few more thumps, grunts, cries, and crashes I couldn't stand it. I didn't want anyone to get hurt.

I slipped on the robe and lunged toward the door, flung it open, walked past the struggling ex-lovers, heading for the only other door, the only other sanctuary in the one-bedroom apartment – the bathroom – saying, "Bring me my clothes," in a take charge way.

"It's the wife, it's the wife," Arlene shrieked again. "I knew it."

"I'm not married," I said to Arlene.

"How long has this been going on?" she screamed.

"I'm leaving," I said to Agnes.

"No," said Agnes, grabbing me. "She's leaving."

"I'm not leaving."

"No."

"Yes."

"No."

"I'm so sorry, baby," Agnes was whimpering to me.

"She's 'So sorry, baby,' " Arlene screamed, emphasizing the word "baby", in fury and hurt. "She's so sorry. What about me?" she wailed. "Why aren't you sorry for me?"

"Bring me my clothes," I said firmly and closed the bathroom door. Agnes passed me my clothes. I knew she would. I seemed to be the one in control, the one with no feelings.

I dressed and then I came out. The fight was out of them. Agnes was sitting on one couch, Arlene on another. Arlene glared at Agnes like she wanted to kill her. Agnes sat with her head buried in her hands looking at the rug.

I had an impulse. I sat down next to Arlene. I believed if I could make eye contact with her, it'd diffuse, it'd be over. Arlene wouldn't try to kill Agnes, or hurt her or herself anymore. Arlene didn't move. Except to turn her head my way. We looked at each other. We made eye contact.

"Arlene," I said. I wanted to take her hand, but didn't. Maybe if this was twenty years ago and we'd all been tripping . . .but I knew the humiliation of this betrayal was tormenting her.

"Arlene. This hasn't been 'going on' " – I made air quotes – "a long time. Not behind your back. It's only been a little while. Since you and Agnes broke up."

But I didn't want to get too precise. It then occurred to me that maybe they had never broken up.

Arlene didn't say anything, but I thought it registered. I got up.

"Don't go," said Agnes.

"I'm going home."

I got up, walked out. Now what? Jack wasn't expecting me for two days. I'd been too convincing a liar. I wished I hadn't taken the car. I was too shaky to drive.

Jack was still up. He was shocked.

"What happened?"

But he was grinning, a happy man. I mumbled something. My bogus excuses came undone easily. I was happy too, glad to be there. It still felt like home. I vowed never to see Agnes again.

I called her the next morning, from the phone in my little writing room with the door closed, wondering if Jack could hear. Agnes sounded terrible. She said she and Arlene talked after I left, calmed down. Arlene went home, more accepting of the split. Agnes cleaned up.

"Did you fuck?" I snarled. I knew Agnes didn't approve of that word. She liked "get laid."

"No."

"I thought you were so strong. Why didn't you wrestle her to the ground? I heard all that struggling, like she was winning."

"I am strong. I knew I could overpower her so I held back."

Her reasoning made me furious. "How come she had keys? I thought you took your stuff back? Why didn't you take your keys back when you took your sweaters?" I said in a small voice, so I wouldn't sound as angry as I felt.

"I didn't want to hurt her feelings."

I wanted to explode, but I didn't feel I had the right to complain.

"Well, it's over now," I said, instead.

"No. It's not over," said Agnes. "I have a feeling it's not over."

It wasn't. But soon after it was over for us, me and Agnes. She was so traumatized by the scene with Arlene and the hurt she caused her that she said we couldn't see each other anymore as lovers. I was glad in a way. Then she got a new girlfriend. It was Candie Boxx.

It wasn't over for me and Jack either.

As the summer ended, I knew I needed to do something before school started. So I put phase two into motion by saying to Jack that I wanted to have a place in the city where I could work. I said I would share it with another woman from school who lived in Montauk and wanted a pied-à-terre of her own. This was partly true. This woman existed. But she did not know about my plan. And if she needed a pied-à-terre, she didn't know it yet. She had a six-room duplex on Central Park with a husband and two sons.

I was so blocked I didn't even discuss it with my therapist, or even tell her that I'd rented an apartment. I'd taken the first one I looked at – a closet for almost $1,000 a month, ground floor, in the front, on the noisiest street in Greenwich Village. I told him the story about sharing it with another instructor from school. I'd mostly use it when the weather was bad, or as a place to work between classes. He could use it too, I said, which was another lie.

That moment coincided with our Soho landlord sending us a contract and offering us money to give up the loft if we were going to stay in Brooklyn. When Jack said, "Well, what do you want to do?" I said, "I never want to go back to the loft, I never want to live there again."

I meant I never wanted to go back there with him, I meant I don't want to live with you anymore. But instead of telling Jack that I wanted to separate, that maybe he'd want to go back there or that maybe I should go back there and live by myself instead of staying in that stupid apartment, I said, "I don't want to live there anymore."

If only Jack hadn't resented my students living in the loft he might have suggested letting them stay on for the legal limit, two years. But he loved our landlord like a father, and he thought that if we didn't want to live in the loft again my students shouldn't either. It wasn't the money. The landlord was going to buy us out, but for only $3,000. Exactly the "fixture fee" we paid the previous tenants of the loft when we moved in twenty-two ago. Inflation was not in our landlord's vocabulary. We had this plan that if Brooklyn didn't last, or if Moms went into a home, we'd move to Sag Harbor. I didn't say I didn't want to do that anymore, either.

The day I told him about the apartment was the day I was having the bed delivered. That night he and I were doing something in the city. He suggested that he come and wait with me. The delivery guys were prompt. Then we drove back to Brooklyn.

But the next morning he asked about the bed again.

"When are you going to sleep in that bed? I thought you

just wanted to use this apartment to work? Why didn't you move back into the loft? What do your students need to be getting such a great deal for anyway?"

I could feel it coming. Finally.

"What is it you want?" Jack asked.

"I want a life of my own, in the city. And a life with you, in Brooklyn," I stammered.

He was calm for moment as it was sinking in. But my heart was sinking.

"You can have your own life, if that's what you want."

I felt better. Then he started to shake his head. Then he got red.

"But not with me."

I got really scared when he said that. My anxiety level was almost unbearable, like I was coming apart, but something felt right about it, good, even. At least I was in motion. I couldn't stop it now. It was coming out. I didn't know what I meant to say. I knew I was tired of not saying what I meant.

"So what do you want?" he said again, making me make the move at last.

"If that's the only choice you're giving me," I said, frantically scrambling one last time to turn it around, turn things back on him, "I want to move out."

"I still don't get it? Why didn't you move back into the loft?"

I still didn't have an answer. I don't know if I do now. I guess I had no way to tell Jack the truth. I was still avoiding it at all costs, even the loft. That I didn't want to live in the loft again seemed irrational, but it was real to me because it seemed easier than saying I didn't want to live with him. I was so consumed with myself, and self-denial, I couldn't consider practical matters, especially real estate. I couldn't consider Jack, that he might want to return there. I could only think about me, if you can call that thinking. Jack got it right away.

"How could you leave me stranded here?" he screamed. "How could you let the loft go? Why didn't you tell me you wanted to leave me? How could you think I'd rather stay in Brooklyn with my mother without you? What kind of a life is this for me? What were you thinking? Fuck you. I'm keeping the car."

I called the landlord. I cried. It'd only been a few days, but he was firm.

"A contract is a contract. I gave my word," he said, meaning he'd promised Joe, the guy in the furniture store, he could use it for storage. Joe didn't even want it. I called everyone. The landlord wouldn't budge. Now he wanted $3,000 a month, not $750. Jack was furious. I was miserable. At least we were talking.

We talked. We cried. We ate, we drank. We planned to make the move gradually. I'd use the car, and take my stuff in slowly. We'd part friends. We drank some more.

"Maybe we can get the loft back," I kept saying as we drifted off into our last sleep together. Somewhere, something inside me felt good.

But not for long. At seven a.m. he bolted up in bed and started screaming at me.

"If you don't get your fucking things and your fucking cats out of here by noon I'm throwing you and the cats out on the street."

The part about the cats terrified me. I called Joy, who was used to bailing me out and started stuffing my things into garbage bags. She drove in from East Hampton – it was a weekend – to help move me. I persuaded him to let the cats stay another day.

When I came back for them the next day, he was calmer. As I was running out the door I had a moment of conscience. After every horrible thing I'd done, me ending up with what I wanted and him ending up with nothing, I thought we should talk. It was one more wrong move, another instance of my thinking I was doing the kind thing when really it was the cruellest. I wanted to spare him the humiliation of ever finding out I'd lied to him, so I told him about Agnes.

"There's one more thing. I want to be totally honest."

He made a funny sound. "What."

"Last spring I got involved with a woman. It's over. It's been over for a while."

(That was the truth.)

"Who was it?"

"Agnes," I told him. "But I wanted you to know."

"Did you tell everybody? Does everybody in the world know about it but me?"

"No."

This was true. Even if everybody else in our world did know about it, I hadn't told them. They heard it through the grapevine. Everyone knew the story of Arlene breaking in on me and Agnes in bed, because the first thing Arlene said, the next day, after she woke up, surrounded by friends, loved ones, and the entire Downtown art world, was my name.

"You could have told me then," Jack said.

"I know," I said.

"We could have worked that out," he said, sweet and sad.

"I know."

I felt bad. I could have had my two lives.

# *Hook*

From the beginning, I wanted to get to Jason Hook, but put it off and off out of fear. Jason, or Hook as everyone called him, was the archivist for the whole crowd and period. He lives by himself, at the moment, in a small house in Montauk, is on the short list for curator at several local museums. He writes about and documents the scene, or what's left of it, from behind the scenes and runs studio tours of all the famous barns and sheds, collects all the materials, does benefits, talks, shows, parties.

Hook isn't an artist like most of the people I talked to. And he's a bit too young to have really known any of these people in their heyday. He's a critic, an historian and a theorist, an expert. I was hoping that his being a youngish middle-aged gay man might help. He has an earring. I wished for the first time for a piercing of my own, somewhere on my face, as a sign.

Jason Hook was having a bad day. A bad week, though I didn't know that yet. But I could see it as soon as I walked in. Interns were screaming. His voice was up there too.

"Where's the champagne, get the phone, why haven't you picked up the boxes?"

They were having a benefit that night. The programs had been printed wrong and the complimentary CDs hadn't gotten there. I should've known better than to stay.

"Could I just ask you a few questions?"

"Well, just a few. What are you looking for?"

"Well, I'm interested in the relationship between Lee and Elaine, and I'm interested in them separately too. I'm interested in the social scene out here, you know, the parties they all went to. The gallery scene in New York fascinates me, you know, East Tenth Street, the shift from Greenwich Village to the East Side, from Paris and London to New York. Oh, and the cemetery, Green River Cemetery, I'm interested in the artists buried there. Especially the women artists."

"That's all you want?" he says snottily. "Well, you should talk to Mercedes Matter about the galleries, she knows all about the early days, Tenth Street, Fourth Avenue."

"Oh, I will," I say, scribbling down this name.

"She lives right down the road."

He rattles off more names.

"Uh, did you know Lee and Elaine socially?"

"Yes, I worked with them when I came here. They were both quite old."

"Were you ever with them together?"

"Never. They were never together. They had no connections," he explodes.

It continues to shock me when I hear these words.

"They must have—"

"Just because they were both painters, lived out here, married to big artists, lived in the same town, knew the same people, what gives you the right to assume they had a relationship?"

It all still sounds right to me. Why are all these people making me feel crazy? Why shouldn't they have been friends? But he's ranting.

"It's the stupidest thing I ever heard of. What are you writing? A romance novel? Fiction? You don't go around making assumptions that fit into some pretty little idiotic schoolgirl idea of friendship and parties for God's sake. You're no writer. You haven't done any background, you haven't read anything, you know nothing about the situation, you don't even know if you like their work."

I confessed this to him earlier, and now he's using it against me.

"You come in here and try to get me to tell you things. You're asking all kinds of stupid questions, expect me to spill my guts about this material, which I'm organizing for a book I'm writing. You try to get me to give away secrets, like it's gossip you want, not truth. You don't know anything about me, my background, what I've done, and what I've done for them, how hard I work. I never get the credit I deserve. You're putting me in a very uncomfortable position. What are you even doing here? You're ruining my day."

He stands up and his chair scrapes raw on the beautiful old floor that some artist's wife probably sanded and stained herself.

"Lee and Elaine! How could you even think such a ridiculous thing? Where did you get that idea?"

"It was a reference in a book."

"What book?" he snaps.

"In Elaine's book."

"Elaine doesn't have a book."

"That book of art essays, in the introduction, June Silver says she saw them together coming down Eighth Street."

"June wasn't in New York that early."

He storms across the room and goes to the archives. He knows the book I mean. He has it. He opens it. I follow and stand there trying to read over his shoulder. He shoves me away. He points to a spot in the text where it says June was quoting someone else I never heard of who'd seen Lee and Elaine on Eighth Street together.

"Lee and Elaine friends! That's just such ridiculous bullshit. You're a fool. Get out of here. You're wasting my time."

I feel like an idiot. I'm wrong about everything. My gut is churning. I know I'm going to be sick tonight.

"And you'll never get to talk to the one June's quoting now," he says.

"Why not?" I whimper.

"Because she's dead."


When I get back to Joy's house, I take down the Elaine book and skim the intro again. Hook, of course, was right. It wasn't June who'd seen Lee and Elaine. It was someone else, all a mistake, a dead end lead.

I call Sofia. For the first time I have no hesitation, my distress is too extreme. Partly, since she set up the meeting with Hook I'm nervous she'll hear back from him how stupid I was. And I don't want her to look bad. But I want something else from her, too. And I know in my heart she has it in hers.

She's not home. I leave a message and go to the beach. It calms me. When I come back there's a message from Sofia about Jason having a bad day too, though not why.

"I'll tell you why when I speak to you," she says, her voice as throaty as usual but unusually playful.

She likes to set up these little intrigues. This time it works perfectly. It excites me, playing right into my detecting compulsion. It cheers me up. I leave another message telling her this. She calls back the next day.

"I hope you got over your bad day with Jason."

"Calling you helped."

"You were afraid he would call me and complain about you."

"Yes. No. Not really that. Just that you're so – how protected you made me feel when I felt so stripped bare and made stupid. What an awful day it was for me."

"He was having a bad week."

"It looked pretty crazy when I walked in. What was going on?"

"I'll explain later. I'll send you a clipping from the *Star*. You'll figure it out."

I'm intrigued again. Back on track.

"Well, I have reason to doubt all the premises of my book. But maybe I can turn it into a funny scene. How foolish he made me feel and how foolish it is, when you try to write about history, knowing nothing, going on instinct—"

"—from a personal point of view," she says.

"Maybe it'll be the last joke."

"The hard part for me," Sofia says, "was hearing you say it made you doubt your work."

I get quiet inside.

"And all the things you have to say about art and love—"

"Oh—"

"—and friendship—"

# FRESH DIRT

# Intra-Venus

I haven't been back to Green River since Joy closed her house last fall. Now, after all those decades of being ignored, my invisible women are starting to get famous.

Hannah's new-found visibility is less of a shock. She has a show coming up at Ronald Feldman, her second show since she died. The first one – the "Intra-Venus" show – she was working on when she was sick, of her being sick – had been at Ronald Feldman the year before. And there was a big group show – "Sexual Politics" – at the Armand Hammer in Los Angeles this summer. I didn't see it but Stella sent me the catalogue. I was excited that Hannah was in it so much, but the show was subtitled "Judy Chicago's Dinner Party in Feminist Art History." It made me think I should go out to Green River again immediately to see if I could find evidence of Hannah having turned over in her grave.

But I didn't go. Back in the city, on my own, I couldn't write. I couldn't finish my book. It was slipping away, and I didn't know how to end it.

I'd been feeling good otherwise. I have new friends in the

city, but now I decide to go to the Ronald Feldman show by myself – to make it more intimate, to think less, and look and feel more. I've been so focussed on Lee and Elaine I lost my connection with Hannah. I realize I miss her. Hannah's real for me. Though annoying when alive, she was my generation. She was vocal about her frustrations about not being recognized, brave and brazen in a way I'm trying to learn from.

This new show is all naked shots, no cunts but lots of guns, some videos from Philly, Hannah stripping behind Marcel Duchamp's "The Bride Stripped Bare," and also "The Large Glass" made for German TV.

Maybe it's the rain from Hurricane Josephine making me feel so wet and cold, suddenly, so alone. I got all choked up when I walked in and saw how pretty Hannah was. Is. There's that forever tense, saved by art. She was really thin then, not puffy like when she was dying. This show is all work from the late seventies, and something about all that time gone by makes me want to cry. We'd lived across the street from each other in our matching lofts. Now that's gone, that life, me in it. I'm still not writing, not really living anywhere, still stuck in this tiny expensive box on Sullivan Street. My cat Josefina died there. So recently, I'm still spooked by it. She dropped dead right in front of me. It reminded me of that time with Iris in the loft. Seeing Josefina rolling around in the bird bra while we were having sex, worrying she'd strangle herself, or have a heart attack. Thinking it'd be my punishment. And now she has died. She died at my feet.

There was a skittering of nails, like a cartoon animal making too sharp and fast a turn. I ran into the little kitchen in time to see her legs go all splayed out. Then she rolled over, heaving before she stopped breathing. A heart attack, just like her brother Stuart. Congenital. I gathered her up, warm, but stiff in a strange way. I put her in her box and ran to the corner, took a cab to the vet. She'd been sleeping in the closet for the last few days, but I didn't recognize it as a sign.

The vet was heartbroken to hear that Jack and I had broken

up. We'd gone through twenty-two years of cats, shots, illnesses, three deaths, together. It made this new death – of this new young beautiful tortoiseshell female cat – all the more terrible.

"There's nothing we can do. She's dead."

It reminded me that Jack had said the same thing about Stuart not that long ago as I sat on the floor in the loft, holding his huge warm paws.

But this time it'd happened right in front of me. I came home from the vet in the pouring rain still stunned and wrung out. And now there's a hurricane named after her.

I leave Hannah's show that same way, stunned and wrung out and sad. I feel lost again, especially walking up Greene Street, where I'd lived in the loft with Jack. And I'm caught in the rain again.

## The Women

Soon after, as I'm reading the *New York Observer* for some gossip about an editor friend of mine, I turn the page to discover, to my amazement, a review of a show called "Women and Abstract Expressionism." I had my typical twin reaction: I felt vindicated and thrilled, pleased for them, like my friends were finally getting recognition; but at the same time I was upset and furious, like someone was stealing my idea.

The review, by a man, said all the wrong things, still focussing on their husbands, on Pollock and de Kooning. The show had just opened at the gallery at Baruch College. I thought about my fantasy show called "Elaine and Lee" that Iris and I and the reinvigorated Guerilla Girls, who would be Guerilla Ghosts, would organize. But someone had done it for me. For them. Not just Lee and Elaine, but Joan Mitchell, Betty Parsons, the gallery owner (I didn't know she was an artist), Perle Fine, Dorothy Dehner, and Ethel Schwabacher, who I'd never heard of. I thought about my doubts, my eager pathetic questions to the people I talked to: Did you like Lee's work?

Was Elaine a good painter? I still didn't know. I couldn't wait to see it.

I walk in. There they are. It's another dark wet cold day. Only my reaction is unexpected. I'm in shock. There is nothing there. Nothing that's beautiful, or powerful as I'd imagined. I feel just awful. Disloyal to Elaine and Lee. But I have to be honest and I honestly feel like it's an awful show: lusterless, colorless, energyless, spiritless, boring. Dead. Is this another joke?

I start to wonder about my obsession with Lee and Elaine. They personified a time in my own childhood, which was their middle period, their peak, and the fading days of the Village, gone before I grew up, turned into a land invented by New York real estate. Now that my life was starting over, I felt like I was fourteen again, when they were there. I made them icons though they weren't then. Now they really were ghostly, slipping away. Besides, Lee was too moral and Elaine couldn't stand to be alone.

I feel sad, worse than when I left Hannah's show, like someone had died, only different. If I could start imagining over, making Elaine and Lee come back as ghosts, give them a second chance, if I could write real fiction, I realize I wouldn't care if they were friends, let alone lovers. If only they could paint.

# *Flash*

Home alone in my tiny apartment, the phone rings.

"Iris?"

"So—"

"How are you?" I ask.

She'd never called while I was out in Sag Harbor all winter and spring. Or in Joy's little house in East Hampton all summer. I get anxious, a familiar feeling. Lightheaded, palms sweaty. Then I feel things I haven't felt in a long time. We'd never talked about "us" or our feelings for each other, or what we'd have had if I hadn't been with Jack. But maybe it never would have worked. She seemed more like affair material. But we'd already done that. I never knew how she really felt about our stopping. Everything was so confusing for me then that I never even knew how I felt about it. I've tried to figure it out since. Regrets? Misgivings? I've had a few. I was attracted to her take-charge no-bullshit style, the way she looked, the way I thought I looked with her. But she was pushy and withholding at the same time. Bad combo. She kept so much in. That was part of the draw. It pulled you in there where you thought all the good stuff was hidden. It's pulling me now, on the phone, in her voice.

"That's not why I'm calling."

"Oh." I immediately feel put down. My stomach starts to knot with a familiar fury. I hated the way she could make me feel. I realize I don't want her at all. Maybe I still wanted her to want me. I want to want, too. But not her. It's like with Grace. I don't want anything old, especially anything connected with the horrible me of the last horrible year.

"Why, then?" I say crisply.

"Were you affected much by the death of de Kooning?"

"Who?"

"De Kooning," she says.

"What?"

"His death? How did it make you feel? How does it affect your book? Do you have to write a new chapter?"

I'm stunned.

"When did de Kooning die?"

The words feel like they're coming out slurry.

"Last week."

"Last week? I don't understand?" I say. How did I miss it?

"How did you miss it?

"How did I miss it?"

I feel awful. Why does it have to be Iris telling me? Why hadn't I called Stella back? Iris's tone seems so mean, punishing. And I'm feeling like I deserve it. All the bad parts of my life seem to glare in the spotlight. If I hadn't been so out of touch with my network of old friends, mine and Jack's friends, many of whom were painters. If I hadn't blown them off. If I hadn't let them all go out of self-defense, fearing they would hate me for what I'd done, to Jack, to them. So many people counted on us to be their life model. Perhaps I feared they'd hate my new life. If I hadn't let messages from my new friends pile up. But I'd started writing again. All I'd done was work and sleep.

"Do you know when the funeral is?"

"No. I figured you went."

"When did he die?"

"About a week ago."

I must've missed the funeral. I can't believe it. The last great piece of the Green River puzzle. In a flash I think of all the lost possibilities: meeting all the people who're still living; seeing a real funeral at Green River, the most important since Pollock's; meeting the daughter, Lisa, and her mother, Joan Ward, all, finally coming together, real, and the real ending of my book, a new last scene I hadn't even imagined. It's disappearing before my eyes. A truly great ending. A real one. Given to me. Handed to me. By fate. And I missed it. I missed it because I was busy finishing my book.

"Well," I said, trying to recover. "I'll make a joke out of it. It's really perfect. My not knowing."

But I feel sick. It's not that simple. My book already has an ending.

The next morning I call Joy.

"I thought you knew. I thought about calling you but I was so sure you knew. I figured you'd gone to the funeral."

"There was a funeral already?"

"Yes. At the Congregational Church. It was last Saturday. It was in the paper."

"The paper?"

"The *Star*. The *East Hampton Star*. I'll save it for you. It said that woman—"

"—Joan Ward—"

"—Yes, she ran it. Then there was an invitation-only reception at Bill's studio on Woodbine."

I'm convinced that if I'd gone to the public service I'd have seen someone I knew who would have taken me to the studio part. I'm doubly miserable for missing it. But she has all the obits, and promises to fax them to me. My phone beeps.

"Would you hang on a second?"

I hit flash. It's Iris.

"Did you find out anything?"

"About what?" I ask, but I know.

"De Kooning."

"The funeral's over."

"You missed it? I still can't believe it. You're such an idiot. We have to go out there. I have to come with you. We have to get the picture. He must be there. Next to Elaine. Come on. I'll rent a car."

"No."

"Why not?"

"It's too late."

"Not for pictures."

"I can't."

"Why not?"

"I just can't."

"You haven't changed."

She hangs up. I feel awful. Joy's waiting on the other line, but I'm so upset that when she asks me if I know about the scandal, I'm too distracted to even ask "what scandal?"

"You should call Sofia. She's in Chicago but she must know everything by now."

"I will, I will," I say defensively, like I'm still talking to Iris.

"Why are you upset? Who was that?"

"A student."

"You give them your number?"

"A former student."

"Call Sofia."

I hang up. I feel too upset to call Sofia, especially in Chicago, but I force myself. Sofia has consoled me so often. But she's out. I leave a message. Then leave the apartment.

I'm fucked up. I feel like all the writing has been for nothing. It's cold out. I come back. There's a message from Sofia. "I guess we'll talk one of these days. Did Joy tell you my piece of gossip from Green River Cemetery? Joan Ward and her daughter Lisa de Kooning don't want Bill buried next to Elaine, so they're keeping de Kooning's ashes in the backyard in that house across from the cemetery until they decide what to do with him, where he should be buried – elsewhere! Some people think they should scatter his ashes, but in the meantime he's just sitting there, waiting. A cause of great concern and gossip in East Hampton, according to my friend Joanna. She must have gotten it from Jason Hook – though maybe it's common knowledge out there. Maybe you should get the recent edition of the *Star*. People will be writing letters about that, that de Kooning should be buried in Green River Cemetery. But if Joanna heard it from Jason, he may not like that I'm spreading the word. So keep it for the book."

# Fresh Dirt

The next morning I feel less discouraged. I'm almost happy. For the first time in a long while, I feel that old pull. I have to go back to Green River Cemetery. Maybe I'm pulled to Green River because it's where art and real estate forever combine, and, considering it's East Hampton, it's dirt cheap. I rent a car. I even book a motel room for two nights. I go directly to the cemetery, even though it's already getting dark.

Maybe I'll find Bill's fresh dirt, like in the beginning, with Hannah. Maybe I'll be the first one to notice, like when Elaine's stone disappeared. Maybe I'll solve this last mystery, I'm thinking as I pull into the back, like the first time I came here, more than three years ago. That day right after Hannah's funeral, looking for her new, still-wet grave with the still-fresh flowers, no headstone yet, just that little bronze placecard. Now she has her permanent arrangement – a big new white marble stone with an etching of an angel – Hannah with wings – a drawing she'd sold to the Museum of Modern Art as a Christmas card. Her sister doesn't like it. And she doesn't like it that Hannah's buried in Green River Cemetery. She wanted Hannah buried in the family plot in the Bronx.

I walk up the hill to see if Willem is there. I pass Lee and Jackson, knowing he certainly won't be near them. I get over to Elaine. There's nothing new next to her. I roam around the whole cemetery, looking for earth recently disturbed, or some new big ornament.

I pass Frank and the others, Ad Reinhart, Stuart Davis, A.J. Liebling and Jean Stafford, James Brooks, Wilfred Zogbaum, Jimmy Ernst, Perle Fine, Harold Rosenberg. I wander back down to the new part and over toward Steve Ross's family plot. I still don't know much more about Steve except that he was head of Time Warner when he died and wasn't gay and that he started out as an undertaker. But there are lots more graves quickly filling up Steve's real estate venture – his new back part of Green River. When I first saw it, his and Hannah's and the four empty reels were just about the only graves. Now it's packed. And the four film reels are no longer anonymous. It's filmmaker Stan Vanderbeek. Another mystery solved, I guess. Henry Geldzsdahler's here now. I heard, from Sofia, that the head of the Fine Arts Deptartment at my school wanted to be near Henry but the only plot near him was too close to the road so she switched it.

As I wander I notice all the artists have little stones on them. I suppose other visitors must have wondered, like me, what the deal was with the little stones. They saw them on Lee Krasner and Hannah Wilke, and Ad Reinhardt, and Harold Rosenberg, but not knowing either, they must have decided that you should put little stones on the graves of artists, as if all artists are Jewish.

It's full dark now. The country always gets a little frightening at night, especially when you're used to street lights. Alone, in the dark, in a cemetery, I start to feel really frightened. I think I'm going to pass out. It's only the third time in my life I've been in a cemetery at night and the other two times I'd been involved with sex and drugs. But to my surprise, it turns out not to be as cold and dark as I expect, especially once I start to move around. Then a car pulls into the back. I think I'm going to faint again from anxiety at the thought of getting caught standing on Steve Ross's mother's grave. I duck down and keep very still. The car is not the cemetery police – probably two people who want to be alone. They see my vehicle, but not me, make a slow U-turn, crunch over the gravel and pull out.

I sit on the ground, then lie down to look up at the stars. For a crazy moment, I'm considering trying to sleep here. I roll over on my side and pull up my legs like I always do in bed, then reverse sides. I'm restless but not afraid. Not lonely. Happy alone. I'm nervous I won't be able to fall asleep. It was sort of the same feeling I had when I was in bed with someone new – Iris or Agnes – but maybe that was guilt, because of Jack. I still hadn't slept with anyone else or found someone I really wanted. The thought of entanglement still makes my stomach churn.

Fog wisps start to drift in, hovering like cartoon Caspers. When a bunch of them brush up together, it's too close – to the image I used to have of Willem visiting, hovering around, to when the rusty old brown Polaroid of Elaine's stone started to fade, too close to the blurry photo Hannah's sister gave me, the one of Francis Ford Coppola and me before our prom – for comfort. I'd imagined the blurs – Francie and Elaine dancing at their Green River prom. Only this time it looks like Elaine and Lee. Are they dancing now? I feel the fog wisps brush my face. The wind comes up in whispers.

"Pssst."

"Elaine?"

"Lee? Is that you again?"

"Again? Who . . .What—"

"Over here!"

"Elaine! How the hell are you?"

"Where the hell are we? I can't believe we keep meeting like this."

"—at our show. I thought I saw you—"

"Saw?"

They laugh.

"Well, felt . . ."

"Smelted?"

They laugh more, moving closer.

"Now here again. What's going on?"

"I felt the earth move—"

"Again?"

They laugh, again.

"It's that girl," Elaine says. "She's the one who keeps bringing us back."

"The writer?" Lee says. "There you are again. The one with the smart answers."

"She hated our show."

"What does she know?"

"Maybe she's right. It's not my best work, Elaine, let's face it."

"I always liked writing better anyway. I just felt I had to, in those days, be a painter."

"Well, your drawing was always superb. You could draw."

"Drawing is more like writing."

"That painting with Bill drawn in, she liked that one."

"Yes. And she wasn't sure she didn't like yours."

"Yes, I felt that. But, you know, Elaine, it was a terrible show. Badly hung."

"Bad choices. Stupid idea, lumping us all together. Just because we're women."

"In our day you painted a show. There was a famous weekend when I had Clem Greenberg and his wife for the weekend, and he was to look at my work. This was when he was with – there was a gallery there that was in the building with French & Company – what was that gallery?"

"That David Smith showed at?"

"That one, yes. I was supposed to show there. Clem was guiding them. So he came to look at the work, and he didn't like it. I was utterly enraged. I had painted the whole show, like I always did after Jackson died. I would go into his studio, put up a whole bunch of blank canvas, and paint a show."

"Do you think anyone in history ever did that before? Had people done that?"

"I don't think so, but that's how we all did it. You painted a show."

"Yes. That was new."

"So I had this show painted, and it was still hanging right where I did it in Jackson's old studio. And Clem went in and didn't much like it. You know, after all, he was the arbiter. He was the one that was going to put it up on the walls or not."

"Wasn't that the weekend Clem got bitten by a dog?"

"You knew?"

"Oh, Lee. Everybody knew everything."

"Well, you knew everything...And everyone...except, maybe, me—"

Elaine sounds serious. "Oh, I always knew about you...I knew you must have been seething."

"Like a volcano."

They both laugh. I can feel their breath.

"So we went to the beach, to diffuse, you know, because I could tell he did not like my work, but I was trying to be a good hostess."

"You were always a wonderful hostess." She clears her throat. It comes out funny. Not a real sound, but we all know what she means.

"I should have invited you more."

"I probably would have refused. But go on."

"We went to the beach. Two dogs attacked each other, and Clem Greenberg interceded—"

"—which you don't do—"

"—and got himself bitten on the wrist."

"Oh, how stupid!"

"How revolting! He's got this big gash on his wrist, he's bleeding all over everything!"

"Horrible."

"Critics!"

They laugh.

"And—"

"He left. He left prematurely that weekend and we were never together again. He'd been very sweet to me, though. At Jackson's funeral, he kept me from falling into the grave."

"Were you at my funeral?"

"Didn't I die first? Funny. I don't remember your funeral. I don't even remember my funeral."

"Well, I don't think you're supposed to."

"You're right. Again."

"You and I should have stuck together. We had much in common."

"You mean Ruth Kligman."

"Yes, that too. But besides Ruth."

"Those other women, our friends, they were too afraid of us."

"We had more drive. Not just because of our husbands."

"No. But we understood their power and attached ourselves to it."

"Speaking of attachment—"

Lee giggles.

"What?"

"I know what you're thinking."

"The four-poster bed—"

"Amazing."

"The realtor—"

"What a riot."

"Did that really happen?"

Lee throws her arm over Elaine and leans in and whispers in her ear, "You know, Elaine, baby, you're quite a performance per ounce."

"You're something else."

"Remember, in the early days, you and I used to meet for coffee—"

"—at Bickfords—"

"Where else?"

"Yes, and one day, afterwards, coming down Eighth Street, someone took our picture. We both had copies. It was a great picture. We could have stayed friends."

"We had other things to do, battles to fight. It was hard enough competing with our husbands. We couldn't have taken on another strong competitor. We thought art was the most important thing."

"The only thing."

"Now I'm not sure."

"You know, she was almost right about us, that girl."

"About us being friends, you mean? I know, and all those people made her feel so stupid, poor thing. I feel sorry for her."

The whispering is all around me.

"I wonder where that picture is now?"

"Wait," I call out. "It's here," I say, reaching out against my will.

I hold out my hand, but as it hits the night air there seems a great white hole, and instead of the picture getting clearer like it's supposed to, in time, the white hole gets bigger and bigger until the whole thing is quickly disappearing before my eyes. What's going on? How could this be happening to me? To us?

Then I remember something strange that happened around my mother's funeral. When she was dying, which took six months, I cared for her. I went every day. And then went home. And came back in the morning. And in between there was always a tiny clock ticking quietly through the anxiety in my head, waiting for the phone call.

Before my mother was totally bedridden, one of the things I used to do for her was take her downstairs to have her hair done. The salon was in her building, on First Avenue, between

Eightieth and Eighty-first St. Every time I went in there with her, Jerry, the stylist would say I wish I could get my hands on your daughter. My mother would agree, and I would get embarrassed. At that point I was cutting my own hair, rarely: it was long and curly and messy. As my mother got sicker, it was looking more unkempt. I never looked in the mirror anymore. Every time he saw me, he said I wish I could get my hands on you. The battle escalated. My mother became more insistent. I became more closed down, returned to an adolescent fury at being told what to do with my hair by my mother. The day she died I waited eight hours for the doctor to come so he could sign the death certificate so the funeral home could bag her and take her away. Just as I finally left her apartment I caught sight of myself in a plate glass window. I looked like a witch. So I called and made an appointment for the next morning with Jerry. I told myself it wasn't to please my mother. I just wanted to look good at the funeral. Anyway, I wanted to tell him that she died.

He gave me a good haircut, not too drastic. It held up well, and I did look good at the funeral. No one said I loved your speech, or you organized the event so well. They all said, oh I wish your mother could see your hair. At first I was enraged but after a while I started saying, maybe she can. That shut them up.

"Lee! Do you see what I see?"

I turn to look.

"Bill?" Elaine calls out. "Is that you, baby?"

The atmosphere around us shifts, a cloud taking a stroll, approaching, on the wind. I see it, too.

"Don't you see? He always did that, took walks in the cemetery at night, after Joan was in bed, to visit, he said, his friends."

"I didn't know he died."

"Nor I."

I feel better.

"Maybe he's coming to visit us."

"Let's hide."

They disappear, but their whispers linger. What they said about using their husbands' power makes me think about Hannah and Oldenburg, and Ana Mendieta and whatshisname.

"—Carl Andre."

"Who said that?" I must be losing it, talking to myself again. But the voice sounds so familiar, whiny, nasal, urgent, and smug. Like Hannah's. I turn and think I see a flashing image – like a slide on a screen in a darkened classroom, of Hannah, then as if reflected, another image of Hannah, pale against the night, lit up in a ghostly way, behind the projector. Two Hannahs showing pictures of herself to her young freshmen students, naked in both places. I can almost see the goosebumps from the cold, foggy night air forming on her long, beautiful arms. They are the arms she had in the seventies, all along, till the end when they puffed up. She looks good. Young in death. Write about me, she says, and drifts away, before I can catch her.

I remember when I started making jokes about Lee and Elaine coming back as lesbians, one of my writer friends thought I should end up having sex in the cemetery with Hannah, a kind of double date, but I couldn't picture it. I couldn't imagine Hannah keeping quiet long enough. But I have to follow her now. I go after what still looks like her naked form lit up by a slide projector beam moving around the cemetery. Can it really be? Every time I think I'm getting closer, the shimmer slips away.

I start up the hill, toward Jackson's huge stone looming in the strange beam of light streaming behind "her." But as I get closer, I see that the big stone isn't Jackson's but Lee's, set right next to his. But what catches my eye is that on top of Lee's stone, so high I can barely see them, are not the little stones that would forever remind me of *Schindler's List*. They aren't stones at all. They are Hannah's little signature bubblegum cunts. Stuck in one of the gum sculptures is a little scallop shell, like the one from a picture I'd once seen of Lee on the beach naked with just a scallop shell over one nipple. She had an incredible body.

I move over to Elaine, now lit up by the old school projector. Her stone looks different, too. The big ugly swirly green thing is gone and in its place a very large pink vagina shape also made of gum. It matches the pink of the stone.

I can't help looking for evidence that Willem was recently buried next to her even though I know he wasn't. I want Elaine and Lee to be side by side even more, but I guess Lee has to stay with Jackson. It seems sad that Elaine, the popular one, should be alone. Elaine should have some connection with him. She did take his name.

"Bill?"

Out of the corner of my eye I notice a big black space. The huge Stuart Davis black monolith is missing. Good for him. He always hated the country. I keep on moving, following the bubblegum, the shaft of light. Harold Rosenberg has no Hebrew on his stone, though for a moment it looks like his grave is crowded with shapes, a crowd of younger women. They're yelling at him. Every time I pass a woman's headstone, there are more little pink bubblegum cunts stuck all over them, not just Lee's and Elaine's, but also Perle Fine, May Rosenberg, Jean Stafford. Not the men. Well, maybe. Frank. I'll see. At first I think they're a kind of defacement, but now I see them stuck all over the women, like Hannah used to stick them all over her body. I finally get it.

The whole cemetery looks different. A red fox runs across the grass, stops in the light, its tail straight out. I look down. There, next to Frank is a new stone. It's Betsy Westgate's, her name, with a birthdate and a waiting dash, like she wished. The grass is bright green. In between them there is a fountain. Someone figured out how to keep it wet.

"Bill?"

Behind Lee and Jackson, now with same-size big golden boulders, all these black vines have suddenly grown in, making a wavy lace curtain behind them, like they said it used to be. The place looks huge.

But the whispering has stopped. The two beautiful clouds above me are sweeping away. A wind has come up, making it warmer not colder, and the other clouds part and drift, leaving stars. I feel calm. I can go now. I get back in the car and turn it around. I start to pull out. When I turn on my lights, as I'm about to give it some gas and drive away, I catch a glimpse of something in my brights, a little cloud, sparkling like tiny particles of floating ash, hovering, caught in the beam.